He's inherited the title of rake. She hides behind her independence... Fate accepts the challenge.

Grace Beaumont has seen what love can do to a woman. Her mother sacrificed her life to produce the coveted son and heir. A devastated father and newborn brother force her to take on the role of Lady Boldon at the age of fifteen. But Grace finds solace in the freedom and power of her new status.

Christopher Roker made a name for himself in the military. The rigor and pragmatism of the army suits him. When a tragic accident heaves Kit into a role he never wanted or expected, his world collides with another type of duty. Returning to England and his newfound responsibilities, the Wicked Earls' Club becomes a refuge from the glitter and malice of London society but cannot ease his emptiness.

Needing an escape from his late brother's memory and reputation, Kit visits the family estate for the summer. Lady Grace, a beauty visiting from a neighboring estate, becomes a welcome distraction. When the chance to return to the military becomes a valid possibility, the earl finds himself wavering between his old life and the lure of an exceptional—and unwilling—woman.

Other Books by Aubrey Wynne

Rolf's Quest
(A Medieval Encounter #1)

Dante's Gift
(A Chicago Christmas novella)

Saving Grace
(A Small Town Romance #1)

Just A Girl Next Door
(Small Town Romance #2)

Merry Christmas, Henry
(A Chicago Christmas novella)

Pete's Mighty Purty Privies
A Just for Sh*#$ and Giggles Short Story)

To Cast A Cliche
(A Just for Sh*#$ and Giggles Short Story)

The Earl of Sunderland

By
Aubrey Wynne

Dear Renate,

Just a token of
my sincere appreciation
for your support.

Aubrey

ISBN-13: 978-1-946560-05-6
ISBN-10: 1-946560-05-7

Editing by The Editing Hall

Cover Art by Taylor Sullivan, Imagination Uncovered

Formatting by Anessa Books

Praise for Earl of Sunderland

"Best Regency Romance I've read in a long time and highly recommend!"

N.N. Light Book Heaven Reviews

"What a grand and delightful story. 5 feel good stars!!!"

Amazon Verified Purchase Review

"A wonderful romance!"

5 Kindles Review

"I adored this story. I look forward to reading more in this series."

Reads2Love Review

Dedication

My sincere thanks to the talented authors of the Wicked Earls' Club for the invitation to join this series. Tammy Andresen and Dawn Brower did a superb job creating the perfect backdrop for our Regency tales. Some are sweet, some are spicy, but all are deliciously romantic.

"The life of the dead is placed in the memory of the living."

Marcus Tullius Cicero

Prologue

March 1810
Northern England, Boldon Estate

The thick air, putrid with death and stale smoke, rebelled against her throat. Grace swiped desperately at the perspiration covering her own face then wrung out the cloth and gently sponged Mama's neck and chest. She couldn't stop the blood flowing from her mother's womb. She couldn't stop the snowstorm that heralded its final revolt against spring. She couldn't stop the tears that washed away her last shred of hope. There would be no doctor, no last minute reprieve.

"Mama, can you hear me?" She closed her eyes against the outrage. Childbirth had been vicious to a woman of her late age, a woman who loved her husband so completely she had risked her life to give him an heir. After almost two days of labor, the reaper had come to claim his prize.

"Gracie?" The countess opened pale blue eyes, her hand fumbling along the bed cover. Grace laced her fingers through her mother's limp ones, the paper-like skin cold to the touch. She glanced over at the fire that blazed and crackled in the hearth.

"I'm here." She leaned close and kissed Mama's cheek. "Please don't leave us. Not yet."

Lady Boldon smiled weakly and shook her head. "I need to see him once more."

"Papa went for the doctor. He's not back yet." She looked again at the white menace pelting the glass panes. "Try to drink something."

Her mother shook her head again. "My boy. I must see my baby boy." She squeezed her daughter's hand. "Please…"

With relief, Grace realized it was not her father needed and went to the corner of the room. She looked down at the healthy, sleeping infant who had stolen Mama's strength. The wet nurse had fed him then bundled him into a white quilted gown. He scrunched his tiny face in irritation as she lifted him from the cradle. Without thought, she tenderly brushed the reddened skin of his cheek. Would he feel guilt when he was old enough to appreciate the sacrifice made for him? Would she resent him for taking away their mother?

Her heart broke again, thinking her brother would never know this selfless woman. She sat on the edge of the feather mattress and laid the baby next to Mama.

"Charles will be so proud of you, my son." Joy shone on the older woman's face as she placed a kiss on the delicate pink skin. "You will make a fine earl someday."

The baby fussed then let out a wail. Grace quickly took him back, not wanting the sound to upset her mother. When she heard a soft knock on the door, she opened it and handed the infant to the wet nurse.

"Let the staff know to send my father up as soon as he returns," she told the servant. "And tell the midwife to hurry with those fresh sheets."

"Gracie!" The urgency in Lady Boldon's voice shot panic up her spine.

"Here, Mama."

"You must promise me..." A ragged gasp was followed by labored breath. "Take good care of my men. They will both need you."

"But *I* still need you." Her mother's face blurred as the tears came once more. "I can't take your place. You can't leave me yet, Mama." Slender fingers gripped Grace's with surprising intensity.

"You're a woman of fifteen now. I've taught you well." She struggled for air. "My Charles will be a lost soul... The baby will need your strength and guidance." Her head fell back against the pillow. "Promise me."

Papa, where are you? Hurry! The words screamed inside her head.

She crawled onto the bed and wrapped her arms around the limp body, gathering comfort in a final embrace from the woman who had seemed invincible. Grace laid her head against her mother's chest. As the death rattle grew louder beneath her ear, she promised. Cold lips brushed her forehead in response.

"Be brave, my darling. Remember, I love you so." With a final shudder, Lady Boldon let go of life.

"It isn't what we say or think that defines us, but what we do."

Jane Austen, *Sense and Sensibility*

Chapter One

Early May 1814
London, England

Lord Christopher Roker slapped his twin brother, the Earl of Sunderland, on the back. "A fit of the blue devils on your wedding day, eh? Come now, the bride seems a prime article to me."

"She's not the woman of *my* choice. I'm more than an unwilling groom. I'm downright defiant." Carson tucked his white linen tails into the pale gray pantaloons, gave his matching waistcoat a tug, and adjusted his neckcloth again. "Yet our parents are deliriously happy over the match because she is the daughter of the Marquess of Landonshire."

"You made your own name." Christopher shook his head and gave his brother's shoulder a hard squeeze. "Gambling and womanizing has its place when you're more boy than man. By Christ, we've passed thirty."

"How did I know I'd fall in love and my reputation would haunt me?" Carson walked over to a polished oak side table and poured two glasses of brandy from the crystal decanter. He handed one to Christopher. "Or that the woman who stole my heart would have a self-righteous father who despises me?"

"How many times did I warn you to pull back on the reins? There are always consequences to one's actions. You will be the Marquess of Falsbury in your own right someday. It's time you accepted some responsibility." He took a sip of the amber liquid as Carson downed his in one gulp and poured another. "It's a bit early for that, isn't it? You might want to pace yourself."

Sunderland sank heavily into a chair, pushing his fingers through a tangle of black waves. "Kit, trade places with me. Marry the chit and take the title. You should have been the heir anyway. You're better suited to this type of life than I am."

"We had this conversation when we were twelve, and you wanted to be a sheik and live in the desert. And then again at sixteen, when you wanted to run away and join the Royal Navy." He smirked and sat down opposite Carson. "Besides, Mother would know at once."

"She'd stay quiet for her darling Christopher. You've always been her favorite." He tipped back his head and gulped the second glass of brandy. "A little courage for the ceremony."

"There will be plenty of time for that afterwards."

"I've missed you, brother. I'm jealous of the army and your long absences." He gave Kit a crooked grin. "It's always been you and me against the world. I don't like having my other half missing."

"Well, I'm here now! Bonaparte is no longer a threat, and we can enjoy a summer in the country this year." A knot tightened in Kit's stomach. He had a bad feeling about this union but knew better than to admit it. It wasn't the wedding itself. Lady Eliza was a beauty and came with a generous dowry. And he didn't believe for a moment Carson loved another woman. Infatuation was more likely. He fell for one chit, and before he hit the ground, another had taken his fancy. While Kit loved his brother, he also accepted his faults. His abilities did not include accountability or dependability.

No, it was the girl's father, Landonshire. His breeding was beyond reproach, but his vile reputation behind closed doors was not well known. He kept his wife and daughter isolated on their estate and rarely entertained or brought them to London. Some of the whispers he'd heard from another officer could make a seasoned soldier grimace. Kit had mentioned it to his father, but the man had waved it away as gossip.

"You're dipping too deep, brother," Kit took the third glass of liquor from his twin, recognizing the slight glaze in those familiar chestnut eyes. "Let's get you to the church, shall we? At this rate, you'll be foxed before the end of the wedding breakfast."

"That's the plan, sir. I won't feel those leg shackles I've acquired."

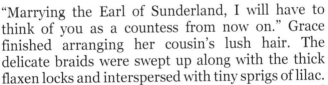

"Marrying the Earl of Sunderland, I will have to think of you as a countess from now on." Grace finished arranging her cousin's lush hair. The delicate braids were swept up along with the thick flaxen locks and interspersed with tiny sprigs of lilac. The pale purple matched the bride's violet eyes and smelled divine.

The wedding dress was of white French muslin, tiny embroidered flowers along the bodice and hem. A pelisse of lavender, trimmed with lace and matching flowers, buttoned just below her bust and amply filled the dress. She had always been jealous of her cousin's porcelain skin and honey hair. Grace had inherited her mother's Scottish looks with a smattering of freckles and the dreaded auburn mane to match.

Eliza smoothed out her skirts again and looked anxiously at her reflection. "He hates me, you know."

"Don't be ridiculous," said Grace, though her nerves had been frayed since meeting the groom two days ago. Something about the earl made her uneasy. Or maybe it was the expectant smile her uncle wore whenever he looked upon his future son-in-law. "He barely knows you."

"Well, at the very least he hates marriage." Tears filled the girl's eyes. "Thank you for coming, dear Gracie. You and Sammy are the closest things to a brother and sister that I have. Mama is practically useless. She is always so afraid to set Father off. I needed someone I could confide in before the ceremony."

Grace bent low and put her cheek next to her cousin's, her own green eyes locking with Eliza's. They were opposites in so many ways. Grace was headstrong, independent, and outspoken. Eliza was docile, compliant, and breathtakingly beautiful. They were first cousins by their mothers and best friends by choice.

Lady Boldon had never hidden her dislike of her sister's husband. *A ruthless scoundrel, that man. He treats women as if they were no better than broodmares*. And Landonshire never hesitated to beat them in the same manner. The law was on the man's side, especially a peer, unless he went too far and murdered his wife or daughter. He was a bitter man who had suffered the loss of several infant boys and his wife's many miscarriages.

"Not all men are cruel, Eliza. Lord Sunderland may not be in love with you, but I see kindness in his eyes. And he's very handsome. If nothing else, consider him a way out of your horrid circumstances."

"Yes, I will keep that in mind." She smiled at her cousin's reflection. "At least I have no bruises to explain on my wedding day."

"I did not come to your wedding for a bout of the megrims. Let me share in your joy today." Grace kissed the bride's cheek and straightened. She pulled back the curtain and looked out the window. "The carriage has arrived. Your parents will be waiting. Are you ready to begin your new life?"

Eliza nodded and turned to embrace her. "You are my dearest friend in all the world. I wish you lived closer."

"Perhaps I could return for a longer stay. Samuel just turned four and may need some distraction this summer. That boy is a constant battle." Grace laughed. "He snuck a pony from the pasture last week and hooked it up to a wagon. Off to battle General Bonaparte with a wooden sword and his trusty hounds."

"If you promise to visit, I'll find plenty of ruffians for him to battle. And you are right. This is my wedding day, and I should enjoy myself." They looped arms, took a deep breath, and descended the staircase with heads held high.

The ceremony was short and somber, and the small party returned to Falsbury as soon as the registry was signed. A larger group had been invited for the wedding breakfast. Falsbury was a regal mansion, and the meal indicated the family's stature. The wedding cake was displayed at the center of the table; the stiff white frosting decorated with herbs and flowers. Ham, accompanied by eggs, hot rolls, and toasted breads, filled the air with mouthwatering aromas. Even chocolate had been added to each table.

Lord Landonshire had watched the young bride and groom with an attempted smile that ended in a sneer. Grace didn't think anything would truly make the man happy. At least he wasn't drinking. Eliza's biggest fear had been that her father would overindulge and show his true colors. But he had toasted the married couple then focused on conversation with several business associates.

Lady Landonshire wore a pleasant, if skittish, expression. Whenever her husband turned to her quickly or moved his hand suddenly, she flinched like a nervous squirrel. The relief in her eyes when he walked away was evident. Eliza had said her parents would stay in London for two weeks. Two weeks of no marks upon her aunt's face. Two weeks reprieve before she returned to her genteel, country prison.

Eliza's flushed face betrayed her shyness and excitement in the crowded room. Her childhood had been lonely, with only visits between the cousins. Experience with the opposite sex had been limited to her father and uncle and the occasional male servant. Grace prayed the wedding night would be...gentle. It would not take much to please Eliza. A bit of civility and consideration might eventually heal her mind if not her heart. *Please God, let it be her time for happiness.*

The groom seemed a bit too jovial for so early in the day. Lord Sunderland drank and toasted a dozen times throughout the wedding feast. An air of self-destruction seemed to hover over him like a storm cloud, and Grace shivered as he pulled Eliza to her feet and kissed her soundly on the mouth. Still, she saw nothing malicious in the man's behavior and considered her cousin better off.

On the other hand, Grace found Lord Christopher to be quite the study of decorum. His deep brown eyes were serious, his black hair combed back neatly, and he cut a fine figure in the red dress uniform of a lieutenant colonel. She found herself picturing him on a charging horse, sword in the air, and a battle cry on his lips. His full, soft lips.

"What has claimed your attention now, my dear?" her father asked in her ear. "Are you plotting your uncle's demise or did some handsome lad catch your eye? "

She giggled then gave him a kiss on the cheek. "You aren't getting rid of me so easily, Papa. Are you enjoying the celebration?"

"Aye, it's a fine wedding. It gives me ideas for other weddings yet to come." He nudged her gently with his elbow, his mouth set in a firm line. "It's time we started thinking about your future. I've been deficient in my duties. Your mother would be mortified to know I've kept you hidden in the country, and you almost twenty."

"I have not been hidden. It was my choice to skip the Season."

"Two seasons, Gracie."

"My home is far more important than socializing with those shallow, silly girls." The thought of standing against a wall, hoping a man would fill her card and not step on her feet during a cotillion, seemed more like a punishment. Making inane conversation while remembering dance steps, and drinking punch fetched by a bored or overeager suitor, was also not a rite of passage that appealed to her. "I'm quite content with my station, Papa. There's no reason to upset our lives over marriage or romance."

Lord Boldon rolled his light brown eyes. "We'll see, daughter. There may come a time you'll eat those fine words." Then he smiled over her head at someone. "Isn't it a grand day for a wedding? Is that music I hear?"

"Indeed, Lord Boldon. I've come to ask Lady Grace for the honor of a dance." A deep baritone sent a warm flush through her belly. "With your permission?"

Her father stood, grasped her hand, and pulled Grace to her feet as she opened her mouth to decline. "My daughter would love to dance."

She looked at her fingers now placed in the man's palm. The heat in her belly began to pirouette and leap toward her throat. When her eyes moved to his face, the dark gaze pinned her to the spot. The air pushed from her lungs, and she found herself unable to speak. A chuckle from her father spurred her to action. With a slight curtsey, she acknowledged her partner, and they joined the others already gathering to the first notes of a country dance.

Grace focused on the gold epaulettes adorning his broad shoulders, as she placed a gloved hand on his wrist. The material did little to diminish the

18 W *Aubrey Wynne*

intensity of his touch as they followed the other couples in a circle.

"I understand you are a cousin to the bride. Are you pleased with the match?" His tone was conversational, but she sensed there was purpose to his question. The group of four came together and separated.

"They make a lovely couple and both families are pleased. Does our opinion matter, my lord?" She risked a peek at her very masculine dance partner as he moved around her. On close inspection, she realized the brothers were not identical as they first appeared. True, their features were the same but their countenances were utterly different. No light-hearted, fanciful expression would ever grace this man's face. She doubted such a proud military officer would overindulge in anything, let alone lose his temper. Control emanated from him.

"No, I suppose not. Forgive my lame attempt at conversation with the second loveliest woman here."

It took a moment for his words to reach her brain as they turned and joined a new set of dancers. They separated again, and when she returned to him, he smiled. Her breath quickened as he spun her around. "You tease me, sir. It is not gallant of you."

"I do not tease, Lady Grace. It is not in my nature." He opened his mouth as if to expand on his nature then stopped. Another twirl and he began again, the smile gone. "Are you enjoying your stay?"

"I did not come for pleasure. That is, I only came to give my support—er, assist my cousin with the wedding. She has no siblings, as you know"—the women moved around the men and came back to their partners—"and she wanted someone close to her own age during the preparations." The couples came together and back out to the rhythm of the music.

"Will you be staying in London long?"

"No, my mother died several years ago, and I am needed on my father's estate. My brother is only four and..."

They split and each moved around the opposite couple. When they were side by side, he picked up where they had left off. "You miss him."

Grace nodded as he twirled her again, surprised at his understanding. "I have never left him before. Never spent a night away from him. I suppose it is how a mother feels the first time she leaves her children."

He twirled her and bent close. "Do you enjoy your role as Lady Boldon?"

His curiosity made her smile and put her at ease. "Yes, I prefer to stay busy and productive." She circled around him. "There is plenty to do on my father's estates."

"A woman stimulated by knowledge. Lovely and clever, a rare combination." He stepped gracefully around her and the other woman of the dance square.

"And are you enjoying your reprieve from the war, now that Bonaparte is exiled in Elba?" Grace had heard of Lord Christopher's fearless reputation on the battlefield. "Do you miss the excitement?"

"No, combat is not a pleasant pastime for me. I miss the regiment and my men, though." He turned her around, and they progressed again to the next group.

"So you will return to your duties?"

"As soon as possible. It is my preferred career choice. I appreciate the organization and logic of the military. We are of a like mind." He chuckled as the couples came together. "London and its society bore me. I *also* like to be productive."

"We have something in common."

"I prefer order, a protocol to follow. Perhaps I'm a skeptic who has seen too much of the world." He stared at her with eyes the color of the chocolate her mother used to drink. They met and parted again. A slight smile still turned up his lips, and she felt bared, as if he was looking into her soul and liked what he saw.

"Perhaps you are also a rare combination of handsomeness and honesty." Her wit had returned, and she found herself enjoying his company. The song came to an end, and he bowed.

"Lady Grace, may I be blunt?"

"Since we've come to know each other so well," she answered with a smirk, studying him from beneath her lashes. He had piqued her interest. "Please, speak your mind."

"My brother has his faults. He drinks too much, gambles but not too heavily, and never takes the blame for a catastrophe, large or small, regardless of his part in it. However, he does not have a spiteful bone in his body and will never, *never* cause injury to a lady." He paused then continued with a slight nod of his head, "I thought you might like to know."

The sun slanted through a window, the bright rays setting fire to his red uniform and making the gold bars across the front glitter. Her heart swelled as she took in his meaning. He knew. He knew about her uncle and wanted to offer some reassurance, some mode of comfort to Eliza on her wedding day.

Tears pricked the back of her eyes, and she blinked quickly before meeting his gaze again.

"Thank you," she whispered, hearing the hope in her voice. "I am very glad to know that."

"May you have a safe and swift journey home. It has truly been a pleasure, Lady Grace." He smiled down at her. A dazzling but sincere smile, showing perfect white teeth that made his tanned skin seem even darker. She shivered, not sure if it was from the heat that rippled over her skin or the improper thoughts that flooded her brain.

"Yes, indeed it has, my lord. May we meet again, someday."

And as Lord Christopher walked away, his powerful stride demanding notice, she hoped they would.

"Seldom, very seldom, does complete truth belong to any human disclosure; seldom can it happen that something is not a little disguised or a little mistaken."

Jane Austen, *Emma*

Chapter Two

Late March 1815
Boldon Estate, northern England

The sound of hoofbeats distracted Grace as she collected a bouquet of pink columbine, yellow daffodils, and snow crocus. The purple and white lilacs would soon bloom and fill the air with the delicious sweet scent of spring. She gathered the lace shawl around her neck, clutched the calico skirt, and hurried toward the terrace steps. Sunlight slanted over the ashen stone of Boldon, casting shadows over the back of the elegant country home. The mansion loomed above her, imposing in its precise symmetry and size. The shade muted the colorful rows of sash windows set in boxes flush with the brickwork. Passing through gardens, she made a mental note to add several herbs to the kitchen plots this year. She smiled and blew at the curl that escaped her bonnet. These months before summer were her favorite, snips of green buds, the scent of amaryllis heavy in the air, petunias pushing up through the earth. New life, new beginnings. And she was hoping for both, or at least a reprieve, after she had a conversation with Papa this afternoon. The thought of being trapped in London when Boldon was so beautiful this time of year...

A horse and rider galloped through the gate. No great coat or cape billowed behind him in the breeze, so she assumed it was a local from the village. There might be correspondence from Eliza. If the visitor was not a post-boy, she could change quickly. The worn chintz was more appropriate for early morning forages than visitors. Not that anyone of status ever arrived unannounced this early. It amused her that morning calls lasted until dinner, when the afternoon sun was already leaning toward the west. Always an early riser, Grace considered half the day gone by the time London society had their breakfast at ten.

As she entered the main hall, Samuel came sliding down the banister from the second floor. "Woohoo, look at me," exclaimed the five-year-old. He unceremoniously plopped onto the rug and looked up at his sister with a grin and a mischievous gleam in his golden brown eyes. "Mrs. Woolley finds the best wax. I must thank her."

"Samuel, I have asked you a thousand times to stop that. What if you fell? Papa would be devastated."

"And you would cry until this mansion floated away, Gracie. You love me more than life itself. You say so all the time." He pulled his knickers back over his knees and moved over to make room for Grace on the third stair.

"Yes, I would indeed cry a river if I lost my sweet brother." She pushed a lock of soft brown hair away from his eyes and kissed the top of his head. He was a replica of his father. "But that does not mean you can run rampant through the estate and cause havoc in your wake."

"How did I manage to raise such dramatic children?" chuckled Lord Boldon. He leaned against the doorframe of the library in only his waistcoast and trousers, observing his offspring. "Tell me such theatrics were inherited from your mother."

"Papa, eavesdropping is impolite," scolded Grace indignantly.

"A man does not eavesdrop in his own house. Anything that goes on under this roof is my business." He folded his arms across his chest as if to drive the point home. "I hate to impose on this touching moment between brother and sister, but we need to finish our discussion, Gracie. My plans have changed for this afternoon, and I need to go into the village."

She bit her lip, his stern tone giving her pause. But her solution was logical and best for everyone, so he must agree. At least it would buy her a little time. "Yes, Papa. Let me give Mrs. Woolley instructions on dinner this evening, and I'll be right in."

"Ten minutes. I will not be put off again."

She gave a silent sigh. Her father would be adamant about her coming out. If he would just hear her out, the compromise would be better for all of them. Oh, why was life so complicated? Why did he believe a husband would make her happier than she already was?

"Did the post arrive while I was walking?" She handed the flowers to the housekeeper, who appeared from behind the stairs. "Please make sure

Master Samuel at least consumes an egg for breakfast. He cannot survive on the worms he tried to eat yesterday."

"If you were lost in the jungle and hadn't eaten in days, you would gladly try a worm." He crossed his arms, the spitting image of his father, and glared at her. "Girls don't understand adventure and survival."

"Papa, we may need a new tutor. I'm not sure I like this emerging attitude." She frowned as her father's shoulders shook slightly, and Sammy hid his face. "What? What is so amusing?"

"Really, my darling girl, you cannot blame Mr. Chenwick." He laughed now, wiping the corner of one eye. "Did you truly think Samuel would eat a worm?"

"I tricked you! I only pretended to eat it," cried Sammy, throwing his arms around her waist. "Papa is taking me fishing at dusk, you goose. That's when the pond fish bite the best. They are for the *fish* to eat, not me!"

Both Grace and Mrs. Woolley shared an exasperated glance and shook their heads. "Well, I'm much relieved to hear it. Now off with you. No studies, no fishing. Do you understand?"

"Yes, ma'am." He skipped down the hall and turned left into the dining room. His high-pitched voice made Grace smile as he instructed the housekeeper on what kind of jam should be on his biscuit.

One male Beaumont content, one to go, Grace thought as she followed her father into the library. He handed her a letter, Eliza's flowing script on the outside. "Oh, I do hope there is good news."

"As in an heir?"

Grace felt the heat rise in her cheeks. "Yes, Papa. It's been almost a year since they were married. She has prayed and prayed for a child."

"It takes more than prayer to produce an heir." Lord Boldon ran a hand over his face. "I apologize, daughter. I'm afraid these long bouts in the country make me forget my manners. But then you look so much like your mother. And there was never anything we could not say to each other in private."

The sadness in his eyes had not diminished whenever he spoke of his late wife. There had been many dark days after her death. Grace had taken on the responsibilities of the house and dealt with her grief as well as the household servants. Her father had sunk into darkness, retreating to his rooms, refusing to see anyone except his children. He held his infant son, cried for the loss of his beloved wife, ranted at the injustice of a god who would take her away. When his tears soaked the swaddling blanket, Grace would retrieve the baby and cajole her father into eating a morsel or two. It took weeks to lure him from his cave of mourning. Once out, his inherent optimism returned, and the wheels of life turned slowly once again. His smile came easier, followed by laughter. That single sound had been the balm she herself had needed to heal.

Lady Boldon had known they would lean heavily on each other. And over the past five years, father and daughter had grown so close they could share almost anything. They had become confidantes of a sort, trying to fill the void of wife and mother for each other in some small way. Grace, however, had been more successful in assuming a maternal role than her father, walking the fine line of affection and discipline with Samuel. It was not always easy telling him no, but it was necessary. She had seen the results of overindulged heirs in London. Arrogant, thoughtless, and selfish. Her cousin Eliza had been forced to marry one such man. Samuel would grow into a kind and generous man if it killed her. An image of herself as a white-haired old lady, shaking her finger from the grave, flashed into her mind. That made her grin.

"What do you find amusing?" her father's question brought her back to the present dilemma.

"That you have brought this on all yourself, Papa. I am what you shaped me to be—proud and independent." Her chin went up, her shoulders set. "You allowed me so much freedom, as if I *were* the lady of the house. Perhaps I would be more eager for a husband if I had not tasted such liberty."

"Don't put the blame on me. The guilt ruse worked for the first two seasons, and I won't hear of it again. We are already late getting to London." He sat on the edge of the huge oak desk and indicated the chair in front of him. "Sit please, so you can't escape so easily. We must look to the future. What will happen to you when Samuel comes of age and marries? This arrangement is fine for now, but his wife will eventually be Lady Boldon. Where will that leave you? I cannot imagine my beautiful, intelligent daughter a spinster living in the west wing."

She sat with a huff and a frown. "I have a plan."

"Of course you do, my dear." He looked at her expectantly. "And what, pray tell, are you scheming now?"

She tried to look indignant, but the grin would not be contained. He knew her too well. "Eliza's last letter invited us to Falsbury Castle this summer before they move on to Brighton. Or were they going to Sanditon this year? I thought perhaps instead of a season in that horrid city, we could spend a month or so in the country. Eliza's mother-in-law, Lady Falsbury, is known for her social gatherings there. Everyone who is anyone waits for an invitation from the marchioness."

Lord Boldon opened his mouth to argue but she curled her fingers around his hand. "I daresay I'll meet just as many eligible bachelors there as I would at Hyde Park or Almack's." This last was said with a wrinkling of her nose. "I hate crowds, and the social events in the country are so much more manageable. Please, Papa?"

Her father drummed his fingers on the desk as he studied the Turkish rug under his polished boots. "So the argument is no longer marriage but the procedure of finding a husband?"

Grace chewed her lip and nodded once. A tiny, miniscule piece of guilt lodged in her throat from the fib. "You promised you would not force me into marriage. And I truly believe those fanciful, frilly gentlemen I met the last time we were in London would never suit me." She peered up her father through thick dark lashes. "I need to find a man who is practical, more salt of the earth. A man like you, Papa."

His chest expanded slightly, a smile brightening his face. "Well, that may be a tall order. But, er, yes. You do not need a dandy for a husband. I quite agree. We'll look for someone who doesn't mind rolling his shirt sleeves up and has more than a passing interest in the operation of his estates."

"We?" Unease poked at her confidence.

"Gracie, I love you with all of my heart. But if I do not take an active role in this pursuit, I will be dead and buried before your banns are read. Now, I will agree to the summer visit under one condition."

The same unease now wound around her lungs and squeezed. "Yes?"

"If we do not find a candidate at Falsbury Castle, you *will* go to London and stay with friends in September. Agreed?"

She focused on the gold swirls in the carpet pattern, her mind racing. If she could convince her father that someone had sparked her interest, London might be avoided. Grace would set her mind to the first task once they arrived, and find a man who seemed to fit the bill. The rest would come to her, she was sure.

"Of course, Papa," she agreed with a dazzling smile. "Your benevolence is more than I deserve."

Let him think he won. Rising with the composure modeled by her mother, she kissed her father on the cheek and moved to the door. Just as she escaped over the threshold, his words smacked her in the back of the head.

"I know your mother always thought her feminine charms beguiled me. But beware, daughter, I have devices of my own."

"Believe me, nothing except a battle lost can be half so melancholy as a battle won."
The Duke of Wellington, letter from the field of Waterloo

Chapter Three

June 17, 1815
Mont St. Jean, near Waterloo

Kit let the slow *drip, drip, drip* lull him, as a puddle formed near his head. Sleep was his top priority tonight, even while battle plans crowded his brain. The rain continued its patter against the tent walls. A thin sheen of moisture seeped through the rough material. He rolled onto his side, his bed at home once again a prized possession compared to the lumpy mattress that provided scant protection from the cold, damp ground. The stale straw and mold would soon be replaced by the sickening sweet smell of blood.

They would fight the French tomorrow. Again. Men would die. Would he be among them? Was this the cause of his anxiety? Fear had never afflicted him before a battle. Now a colonel with years of experience behind him, engaging the enemy still brought on thoughts of mortality but never this eerie foreboding. Fingers of dread scratched up his spine; the knot in his belly pulled tight.

Bonaparte had escaped Elba and retaken Paris. As the new French army multiplied, British Field Marshall, the Duke of Wellington, ordered troops back to Belgium. While waiting in Brussels, the lovely Duchess of Richmond had asked her husband to host a ball as a distraction from the upcoming conflict. Wellington agreed it would be good for morale, and the officers cheerfully attended. The event was a success until a messenger brought news the French had crossed the border and were making their way to Brussels. Kit had heard the duke ask his host for a good map and knew the evening would not end well.

Pandemonium ensued when orders were given for all officers to join their regiment and be prepared to march by three in the morning. Women wailed while husbands, fathers, and sons tried to soothe them. Younger men chattered in excitement with military ardor; orders were shouted above the uproar. The affair had gone from a delightful dance to an utter state of chaos. Kit grimaced, remembering the courageous wives and mistresses who accompanied their beloved. Did they not realize? Cannon and musket fire did not discriminate between male and female.

Then another strange emotion gripped him. Would someone ever love him so much? He focused once again on the rain and drifted toward slumber, but his dreams refused to let him rest.

The smoke wafted around his ankles, glimpses of red appearing in the gray wisps then vanishing. The loud suction of boots pulling from the muck created an eerie rhythm in the foggy surroundings.

Screams pierced the air as frequently as musket fire, and moans drifted up from the muddy ground. The whinny of a horse. Gruff commands barked from the saddle.

He squinted at the movement in front of him. A French soldier ran forward, bayonet pointed at Kit's belly. He dodged, missing the thrust, and brought the back of his rifle down on the man's head before running him through the back. Two more emerged. He put a bullet in one man's head and sliced the throat of the other with his saber. Panting, he looked around for his men and found he was alone.

A white horse appeared above him, rearing on its powerful hindquarters. A shrill cry rang out, followed by a loud thud as its front hooves came down and pawed at the sludge, sending a spray of filth across Kit's skin. As he wiped it off with his coat sleeve, it turned red then dripped onto the gold bars of his uniform. He rubbed furiously with his gloved fingers but the color only deepened to a scarlet and then poured onto his black boots.

"It's coming from me," a familiar voice yelled over the din, a smirk on his face. "Sorry about the mess."

He looked up and saw his own face looking down at him. Blood gushed from the soldier's chest. His head sat at an odd angle and bobbled as the horse pranced. Kit reached up to help his brother off the horse.

"It's too late for me. It's your turn now," came the voice again, sorrow now lacing his tone. "It always should have been, you know."

Grabbing the man's boot, he tried again to pull the soldier down. Instead, a boot kicked him in the *face and sent him sprawling backwards. Hot pain ripped across his back and radiated up his neck as he hit the ground. The huge beast, now riderless, reared again, showering his face with mud.*

"No! No! Let me help you," Kit pleaded as he spit mud from his mouth, arms flailing against wet sludge scattering over his head. "Please…"

Kit cried out, his arms thrashing at the air. His face scrunched up at a bead of water that plunked onto his cheek. Struggling to pull air into his lungs, his mind groped for rational thought. He rubbed the back of his aching neck, stretched the stiff muscles, and peered at the dark stain above him. The rain had wormed its way through a patch of the canvas above his head. *The drips of blood*, he thought as he wiped the cold sweat from his face. He hated bad dreams.

A weak light filtered through a crack in the tent opening. It was almost dawn. Muffled voices and the clang of metal announced a new day.

"Colonel Roker, sir?" A shadow appeared on the other side of the flap. "I have a message from Brussels."

"Yes, enter." He cleared his throat of the gravel that had lodged there overnight. With a heavy sigh, Kit pulled on his leather boots and stood up. His shoulders throbbed as if he had been thrown from the stallion in his dream. A chill passed over him, surreal images flashing through his mind again. The same foreboding from the previous night returned along with the knot in his stomach. Perhaps it was age. He and Carson had celebrated thirty-two years on their last birthday. Right now, those years seemed to weigh on him.

"The French defeated the Prussians at Ligny, my lord. But the field marshal has rounded up the remaining troops and is marching as we speak." The soldier stood erect, waiting for a reply or orders.

"At ease." Kit held out his hand for the orders. Breaking the seal, he unfolded the thick parchment.

Scouts report Bonaparte has not inspected the troops or been on the field today. Possibly due to bad weather. Better footing for cannon. If delay continues, von Bluche may have enough time to reach us from Ligny. Collect your troops and stand ready.

"Spread the word to assemble, Captain. I heard the women up earlier. Make sure you get some tack and ale. We will need our strength today to put this devil in his place."

"Yes, sir." With a salute and slight bow, the soldier exited the tent.

Kit dressed slowly, his thoughts entirely on the men in his regiment. The dream vanished from his consciousness, replaced with duty and the responsibility of hundreds of men under his charge. He prayed most of them would be standing at the end of the day but doubted it.

Bodies lay mangled and bent. There was not a clearing large enough for a medical tent without removing corpses from the field. Kit couldn't begin to tally the fallen. But the Allies were victorious. Waterloo had been the end of Napoleon Bonaparte. Good riddance.

A sergeant chased off one of the local women, hacking at a dead man's finger for his ring. The spoils were part of the incentive of the winning side, plus the prize money from the crown would be sizeable. Kit should receive at least 400 pounds. More villagers bent over the dead with pliers, pulling teeth. These were sold to make dentures and turned a nice profit for anyone who had the stomach for the work. Kit shivered in the warm evening air. Life was hard for many of these peasants, and he was not one to judge. Who knew what callouses had been scoured onto their hearts. But he knew one thing for certain. This would be Christopher Roker's last war.

Home. The word had been ringing in his head since the first battle cry. He'd be back in London in less than a month. His father's scowling face and his mother's hovering image suddenly seemed like a warm blanket he wanted to wrap around himself, and thaw out the ice that filled his bones in the middle of June. Normalcy, that's what his soul craved. To wake up and not have lives hanging in the balance. To watch over his brother and scold him when he overdrank or gambled too much. To have the most difficult decision of the day be a ride in Hyde Park or a boxing match at Jackson's.

Good God, what sentimental hullabaloo filled his head these past few hours. Next, he'd be in a rocker with a blanket warming his knees.

A day later, a courier arrived from London as he prepared to leave Brussels. He had procured lodgings in a hotel and just finished breakfast. When Kit saw the Marquess of Falsbury's seal and his father's handwriting on the envelope, his stomach clenched. Their family did not write socially. Something was amiss, and the nightmare he'd had just before Waterloo dashed through his mind. He cursed his fumbling fingers and broke the wax.

17 June 1805

Dear Christopher,

> *Your mother is too distraught to compose a letter, so the task falls to me. Carson had a terrible accident last night. It seems he was in his usual state after the clubs, and decided to race our fastest stallion at dawn. The beast stumbled, and C. fell to his death. His neck was broken. I do not think he suffered. My only blessing in this dark time.*

> *You must come home immediately. I understand you were brilliant against the French and hope you've had your fill of the military life. You are now the Earl of Sunderland and heir to Falsbury. I desperately need help with the two hysterical females on my hands. Hurry. It's a damnable day when a man has to bury his son.*

Falsbury

His lungs froze. His limbs turned to lead. He couldn't pry his fingers from the paper or his eyes from the ink. The words swam before him.

"Are you all right, my lord?" asked the courier. "I am to take a reply back to the marquess."

Air finally seeped into Kit's chest, and he drew a long, deep breath then let it out slowly. His military training would be sorely needed now. "Go down to the pub and get me a bottle of their best brandy. I will have a response when you return." He tossed the man a coin and waited for the door to close. With a reserve he didn't know he possessed, Kit walked slowly to the writing desk, sat down, and opened the bottle of ink. *Write the letter, and then drink until you're numb. Chin up. Chin up*, his brain demanded.

He composed a short note, telling his father of his shock and concern for the family and that he would depart immediately. When the messenger returned, Kit traded the letter for the bottle and bid the man good day. He removed his uniform and exchanged it for civilian clothes, leaving the linen shirt open and boots off. Then he waited for the darkness to descend.

"Carson, here's to your freedom." The amber liquid scalded his throat, and he welcomed it.

"And here's to finally getting your way." The next glass didn't burn as badly so he measured out a third. "You finally won your battle, big brother."

His resolve ebbed, and he sank into a chair in front of the window. A carriage drove by, people hurried down the street, a dog barked at a nervous horse. The grief was building. It had begun in his stomach and now rose to his throat, expanding and making it difficult to swallow. His jaw clenched, trying to push the pain back down. But the misery would not be ignored. It entered his head, a pounding that forced his eyes closed. Blindly, he threw back another glass of the brandy.

"Work, damn you. I can still feel." The stinging behind his lids brought forth more cursing. "Why? WHY?" A tear escaped, sending him into a rage.

He threw the glass across the room with all the fury of the past week. The snifter hit the mantel and shattered into tiny shards like his composure. Rays of light poured in from the windows, the slivers of crystal winking and sparkling against the deep green carpet. Kit looked accusingly at the bright day, as if the sun had no right to shine.

Conversations whispered in his ear. Schemes to trade places, switch roles. *You be the earl. No one will ever know. You're so much better suited to a title.* What if they had gone through with it? Would Carson still be alive? Or would he have joined the army and gotten himself killed? He might have tried law. Kit snorted, remembering his brother's expert flummery. Yes, a barrister would have suited him. The anger resurfaced.

"How in bloody hell do I live without my other half? Can you tell me that, you selfish bastard?" He picked up the decanter and took a long draw from the bottle then chuckled without mirth.

"You thought I was the strongest. Always the one to bail you out of trouble, smooth things over with our father." His voice broke. "Well, I'm in over my head now."

The decanter dropped from his fingers with a thud, the golden liquid seeping into the carpet as the lifeblood had seeped from his brother. The nightmare had been Carson, trying to explain what had happened. His funny, sweet, reckless brother, looking out for him in his own inept way.

Kit clutched at his chest, at the gash in his heart. Twins were known to have an uncanny bond, and they had been no different. A part of him was dead, along with his brother. It was a grief he knew would never leave him. So he gave into the pain and let it wash over his body. "Damn you, Carson. Damn you."

"But the night-dew that falls, tho' in silence it weeps,
Shall brighten with verdure the grave where he sleeps,
And the tear that we shed, though in secret it rolls,
Shall long keep his memory green in our souls."
Thomas Moore, *Oh, Breathe Not His Name*

Chapter Four

June 1815
Boldon Estate, outside of London

It was the perfect afternoon for a funeral. The weather and his mood had cooperated beautifully. Kit had finally achieved the numbness he'd desired and did not intend to relinquish that particular state in the near future. He studied the small church where he had spent so many Sundays as a child trying to sit quietly during a never-ending service. Carson, never good at sitting let alone quietly, always managed some kind of mischief. One Sunday, Kit remembered the peculiar sound of scratching while the new deacon rambled on nervously about the vices of gambling on horses. The old vicar's sore throat had worsened that morning, and the recently ordained young man had been handed the sermon at the last moment and pushed onto the pulpit.

Carson had taken advantage of the situation and pulled out a small carving blade. Lady Falsbury had begun sitting in the second row rather than the first, so she could pinch her eldest son when necessary. But he had slyly hopped over Kit just as the poor curate began to speak. With the bench in front of him hiding his hands, Carson grinned and continued his whittling. No amount of subtle elbow nudging from his brother or warning glares from his mother impeded his mission.

"What's it supposed to mean?" he had asked Carson before their mother had climbed into the carriage. "Are you trying to get me in trouble along with you?"

"They'd never blame you. It's always me, whether I did or not." His brother had sounded indignant—no, melancholy. It had been one of the few serious conversations Kit could remember. "It was for God. I wanted to remind him that we are from the same cut. So when he has mercy on you, he'll spare some for me. Our parents never listen to us, so maybe God will."

Kit's thumb now ran over the letters C-A-R-K-I-T as he sat again in the second pew, the memory turning his mouth in a sad smile. *I hope you received both our shares of mercy*, he thought. The tears and sniffles of his mother and sister-in-law accompanied the droning of the vicar, who regaled the small group on the wonderful qualities of the deceased. How amused Carson would be at all the fuss in his honor. After the service, Lord Falsbury helped his wife into the carriage. Lady Eliza, in a sudden show of defiance, insisted on going to her husband's grave.

"We had little enough time together as it was. I am not ready to leave him just yet." Her head snapped up and her chin thrust out, making the black veil quiver around her neck. She really was a pathetic creature. So frail and thin. Her heart-shaped face was pale, and the dark circles under her eyes were not hidden by the sheer crape. What kind of relationship had she shared with his brother? He doubted Carson had loved the woman. Yet, the tears and sorrow were genuine. His eyes veered skyward. *Did she touch that heart of yours, brother? Is it comforting to know a woman cries for you?*

He swore something swatted the back of his head. Of course Carson would be pleased someone shed tears at his funeral. He covered his chuckle with a cough and followed the sparse group to the mausoleum. Kit fingered the small gold "W" on his lapel while the vicar intoned yet another prayer. Lady Eliza had given the small pin to him.

"This was on his favorite tailcoat. The one he always wore out with his friends. Sometimes I saw it on his neck cloth. I think it was important to him, so you should have it." She had pinned the letter onto Kit's collar.

He studied the small group inside the family's mausoleum. To his right stood the estate manager and another man he did not recognize. From his dress, the stranger was a gentleman. A flash caught his eye, and he spotted the same "W" on the man's cravat that Carson had worn. Coincidence? He doubted it. His years in the king's army had taught him there were few of those in life.

The praying came to a blessed end and the party shuffled outside into the growing heat. Kit told his father not to wait, preferring to walk home. The exercise would do him good. The life of soldier was not this blasted sedentary.

"Lord Sunderland, may I offer my condolences?" The man removed his hat, revealing a once dark head of hair, now mostly gray. His green eyes offered sympathy. "Your brother was a good man, though a bit wayward. But many of us are."

"Us?" Kit didn't like being at a disadvantage. "And you are?"

"Pardon me, I am the Earl of Coventry. "

"It seems we have a jeweler in common," Kit replied with a guarded smile as rubbed his thumb over the "W" on his lapel. "May I ask what it represents?"

"It stands for Wicked. Wicked Earls." Lord Coventry smiled. "And no, we are not all lascivious rakes, though my club protects the privacy of whatever dark desires my clients may have. It is a discreet membership."

"And my brother was part of this elite group?" Kit raised one eyebrow. "I am not surprised."

"We share another common friend, the Earl of Weston."

"Edward? I've known him since he was knee-high." Kit smiled broadly for the first time in weeks. "By god, I need to get in touch with him. He was a bit younger but managed to keep up with us."

"He was not able to attend today, so I came in his stead. We are getting together next week at the club in honor of the late earl. Reminiscing, sharing stories, that sort of thing." He handed Kit a card with the "W" insignia. "I thought you might like to join us."

Kit took the card, ignored the pang in his chest, and looked sideways at Coventry. "So not all of London thought him a devil?"

"No, there was more to Sunderland than he let on to the *ton*. Still waters and all that..."

"Ha! There was nothing *still* about my brother!"

"No, I suppose you are right. Though he did manage to slow down a bit." The earl laughed and placed his hat back on his head. "Hope to see you next week, my lord. Again, my condolences. Bloody shame."

Kit watched the earl walk away, signaling at a horse and driver down the road. A phaeton pulled up, and Coventry leapt into it with the grace and speed of a much younger man. He wondered about the wicked earls. They couldn't be so bad if Weston was one of them. He hadn't seen his childhood friend since Carson's wedding. It would useful and heartening to have a trusted friend in his corner now that he was home.

When he returned to the estate, his father was waiting for him in the library with brandy poured. "I don't usually partake this early in the afternoon but it feels like it's been a bloody long day," Falsbury handed Kit a crystal glass. "Sit down, son. There is much to discuss and no use putting it off."

Laying his dark tail-coat over the back of a chair, he leaned against the fireplace mantel and removed his cravat. "Where shall we start?"

Falsbury handed him a glass then settled himself behind his desk. "First, your brother had a few vowels left unpaid. I'd appreciate you taking care of those debts as soon as possible."

Kit nodded. "Was he in deep?"

"No, surprisingly. He gambled often but not heavily. Never hung on my sleeve." He stared out the window, a distressed look on his face. "I feel as if it were all wasted time. If I'd known what would happen, I'd have skipped all those confrontations."

"How were we to know?" Streaks of late afternoon sunlight speckled the desk and highlighted the gray in his father's hair. The lines around his eyes and mouth had deepened. He had aged years since Kit had last seen him. "You're right—we are starting over. I don't know anything about running Falsbury or your other estates."

"You will learn. God can't possibly take both of my sons." His brown eyes watered; he turned his head and cleared his throat. "At least you have the temperament for the title. It won't be an uphill battle."

"Yes, I've always been the obedient son. Then again, I haven't been forced to do anything I dislike." He took a sip of the brandy and appreciated the slow burn down his throat. "But I am a man of honor and will do my duty."

"I know you will, Christopher. Perhaps the two of you *should* have switched identities. I know Carson tried to convince you of it." With a heavy sigh, the older man turned back to the papers on his desk. "So many legalities to deal with, I'm afraid. The solicitor will finish drawing up the papers to name you the fifth Earl of Sunderland and heir to Falsbury. The second son is now a future marquess. How does it feel?"

"Bloody awful. The title will take a bit of getting used to, I suppose."

"And then there is Lady Sund—er, Lady Eliza," he added, drumming his fingers on the desk. "I assume she will return home to her family. Her father sent word that he'll make arrangements as soon as we are ready."

"Her father is a demmed sneaksby, you know that." Kit remembered the conversation with Lady Grace over a year ago. "He beats his women. I can't imagine she'll want to go back to that."

The marquess waved a hand. "That's not my concern. She'll have a tidy income until she remarries, so as a widow she can do what she wants. I don't see her having enough backbone to be independent, but as I said, it will be her decision."

"I need to go to London next week, so I can stop at the solicitor's office then." Kit decided his next conversation would be with the widow. "Shall we meet for a set time each day to begin familiarizing me with my duties and your expectations?"

"Always the military man, eh? Even as a boy, you liked routine, everything orderly and kept in its place. But you used to smile more. It was the one thing you and your brother had in common. The war, I suppose?"

Kit grunted. "It certainly doesn't lighten one's disposition, does it?"

"No, I imagine not." His father tipped his head and finished off the brandy. "I feel old today. First time in my life that the years are weighing on me."

"Unpleasant for all of us. If there's nothing else, my lord, I need to check on Mother." He picked up his tailcoat then paused. "Would it have made a difference if I'd been here?"

His father smiled weakly and shook his head. "That's the irony of this tragedy. Carson had come around. No more rumors of him at the brothels or gaming-hells, no revel rousing. He treated his wife with polite deference and even appeared to enjoy her company. I had such high hopes."

When the old man's gaze wandered to the window again, Kit slipped quietly out of the room. Good god, how was he going to do this? He already missed the army. It held a security, an assurance of what the future would bring—if one didn't fall in battle. But that was a price every soldier had to be willing to pay. At his age, how did one start over? Learning how to manage the estates wouldn't be a problem, he reasoned. He managed hundreds of men from all classes. It was the whole marriage and heir predicament. Now he knew how Carson had felt. Except this had been sprung on him like a hunting trap. And there was no escape.

With a knock, he entered the drawing room where his mother sat reading a bible. She was still an attractive woman, her cheeks still smooth and only a few streaks of gray threaded her ebony hair. "Can I get you anything, Mother?"

She lifted her red-rimmed eyes and held out her hand. "A kiss from my son? It will provide me with more comfort than this book."

"Of course," he replied, bending over her to place one on her soft cheek. "Anything else? I wanted to speak to Lady Eliza. Would it be better if you came along?"

Her face brightened with the subject. "Such a sweet, precious girl. She's been great company for me since the wedding. Everything a woman could want in a daughter."

"Do you know if she has made any plans?"

"No. Why don't you ring for a servant, and we'll send for her."

Kit obliged, and while they waited, Lady Falsbury confided she didn't want her daughter-in-law to leave. "If she could stay for a while, it would be such a comfort to have her near until I am...better."

The woman in question appeared at the threshold. "My lord, Lady Falsbury, you wanted to see me?"

"Yes, please come in and make yourself comfortable. We were just talking about the future." He noticed her drawn face, the pinched expression. "Are you feeling up to it?"

"Sit down, my dear," Lady Falsbury murmured as she patted a chair next to her own. "It can wait for another day if you are not quite yourself yet."

Lady Eliza shook her head. "No, I'm well enough. Thank you for inquiring, Lord Sun...Sunderland."

When she faltered over the name, he cringed. "It will take some time for all of us to become accustomed to my title. When we are in private, perhaps it may be better for both of us if you call me Kit."

"Yes, my lord."

"My father is under the impression you will return to your family. My mother is hoping you will grace us with your presence for a while longer. We are in no hurry to see you go." He paused. Her fidgeting had intensified and a perfect crease appeared on the lap of her black dress. "Am I distressing you, Lady Eliza?"

"That will depend on your reaction." She blinked twice then lowered her eyes again, her fingers pulling on a strand of blonde hair. "I fear I am carrying Carson's baby."

Silence. The kind of early morning silence just before the sun bursts over the horizon. And burst it did.

"Oh, my dear," cried his mother, tears spilling from her dark eyes. "Are you sure? You are with child?"

With only a nod in confirmation, her eyes remained pinned to her leather shoes, peeping out from the bombazine skirt.

Surprise attack, punched in the gut. Kit swiped a hand over his face as the implications of this news came over him. A reprieve? Possibly. Did he want to be held at bay? Left dangling here in England while he waited to see if the title would be his or given to a bawling infant? Bloody hell, a complication he hadn't foreseen.

"Lady Eliza, you realize what this means?" he asked quietly. She nodded once again. "Well, may I be the first to congratulate you."

Her head lifted, her violet eyes swimming in unshed tears. "You are not angry?"

To his astonishment, some of the darkness had lifted from his soul. A baby. A nephew. Carson's child. "No, my dear sister. I'm very happy, very happy indeed." He held out his hands, and she rose to clutch them in her own as he kissed each of her cheeks. "That answers one question. You won't be leaving us any time soon."

A tremulous smile grew, transforming her face from haggard to lovely. The women's joy swelled his heart. Yes, this was good news.

"Eliza, what have you eaten today? We need to get sustenance in that scrawny body. My grandson will have a hearty appetite." Lady Falsbury wiped the tears from her face, the pale blue eyes brightening.

"Christopher, ring for a light luncheon, please. I find my appetite has also returned. Oh, fetch your father but have some brandy on the ready."

"There is no charm equal to tenderness of heart."

Jane Austen, *Emma*

Chapter Five

Late June 1815
Boldon Estate

I don't mean to sound harsh, but there is no need to stay with Eliza now." Lord Boldon spread out his hands. "The family will be in mourning with no possibility of entertaining until next season."

"Yes, Papa, but I'm going for different reasons now. I would be with her already if you had allowed me to attend the funeral." Grace gave her father a mutinous look.

He wagged a finger at her. "Women do not have the constitution for such affairs. Lady Falsbury would not have approved. She only attended the church service, and it was her son."

"That's balderdash and you know it. I should have been there for Eliza." Grace was not letting this go, even as the tears stung the back of her eyes. When Mama died, neither her aunt nor cousin had been allowed to visit. She remembered how much it would have meant to her to have Eliza there. "I know what it feels like to be alone in time of sorrow."

She shouldn't have said it. Her hand went to her mouth, and she shook her head. "Oh, Papa. I'm so sorry. I'm such a dimwit. I didn't mean—"

"You did, and you are right. I wasn't there for you when your mother died. I was drowning in self-pity, and you manned the ship until I could steer it again." He held out his arms, and she hugged him fiercely. He held her for a moment, stroking her back. "Oh, my sweet. I worry such a visit will steal the brightness from your eyes."

"I'll be fine. I have come up with a plan."

He chuckled. "Another plan? Please tell me there is a husband somewhere at the end of this latest scheme of yours."

"This is no longer about marriage. Eliza is with child and in mourning. She needs me. Please, Papa, we cannot deny her our love and support when she needs us the most." She held one of his big hands in both of hers. "A woman's worst enemy is her own imagination. With our history in the birthing bed, she will need a trusted voice to calm her fears. Think of your niece. Think of Mama. She would be horrified if we did not do everything in our power to help her sister's only child."

Her father puffed out his cheeks and blew the air out dramatically. "When you put it like that, I see no way to refuse. But this matter is only postponed."

"Yes, Papa. Oh thank you," she gushed then wiped at the corners of her eyes with her palm and stood on tiptoe to kiss his cheek.

As she left the library, her mind whirled with arrangements she needed to make and the necessary packing. There was so much to do.

"Sammy, Sammy, I need your help." She called to her little brother who once again perched on the top of the landing. "And don't you dare ride down that bannister."

With a grin, the little boy gave a salute, lay down on the gleaming wood, and slid to the bottom step. "I didn't fall on my bum this time, Gracie. I'm getting better."

"Watch your language, you impudent child. Now, we are leaving in less than a week to visit cousin Eliza. You need to make a list of what I should pack for you. Not *all* of your toys, mind you, but don't forget anything important."

"Like Thor," he offered. "He would be very upset if I left him behind."

"Yes, you would both be devastated. He would not like to miss this adventure." Thor was Sammy's wooden warhorse. The local carpenter had made it for her mother just before his birth.

"And my toy theater," he added. "I wager Eliza would like to watch some of our plays."

"I'm sure she will enjoy them immensely."

"And my whirligig, I can't—"

"Make a list. Don't worry about the correct spelling or have your Mr. Chenwick help with it."

"I can write my letters all by myself now," he said with lips pursed, eyes scrunched, and arms crossed over his chest. His pout was adorable. When he stomped his foot, the dark blue breeches fell back over his knees.

She crossed her own arms and screwed up her face in imitation. "I remember now why you're so good at plays and drama. Now, get up those stairs and make that list. I won't be responsible if it's not on your list."

Grace was excited to stay at Falsbury for a month but still had a knot in her stomach about the pregnancy. Her cousin's letter had been filled with sadness and joy. She read it again, an intense protectiveness filling her chest.

> *Dearest Grace,*
>
> *This must be a dreadful dream. I will wake up soon and cry with relief, but until then, my heart is breaking. Carson is dead. One moment he is kissing me good night, off to the clubs with Lord Weston. The next, I'm roused from my bed to learn he has fallen from a horse and broken his neck. How will I bear it?*
>
> *I know we were not a love match, but he was so good to me, Gracie. So tender and considerate and like no man I have ever known. Why would God give me such happiness for such a short time? I lay awake wondering if I would have been better off never knowing such affection.*
>
> *My only consolation is his child growing inside me. He made me promise to keep it our secret for awhile. He wanted to savor the moment, he said, before his father sucked the joy from it. He was so happy, and I thought I was the luckiest of women. Now I will have to tell them alone, without him by my side. Oh, pray that I have a daughter, so I may keep her to myself. They won't care about a*

useless little girl, but I would cherish her. A small part of Carson left behind for me.

I need you, Gracie. I need your strength and your common sense. Please come to me when you can.

Your loving cousin,

Eliza

Her first reaction to Eliza's terrible and wonderful news had been tears. Tears for a dead man who had shown kindness to a lonely, frightened girl. Tears for a woman who would now raise a child without his father. Tears for the ghastly possibility the reaper might return and take Eliza from her. And then relief no one had witnessed her breakdown. She had fretted, considered begging off the invitation with a poor excuse. She wanted to offer solace but would Eliza's swelling belly bring back all the fear and horror of that awful day? Her father's concern had not been trivial.

Her apprehension was short-lived, though. Grace considered herself a problem-solver. Whining won't help. Find a resolution, her mother had always said. After extensive reading and long conversations with the local doctor, chemist, and midwife, she found a practical solution. There were now male practitioners that specialized in birthing. Her present mission was to convince Lady Falsbury the baby should be born in London, where an accoucheur could be engaged in advance and sent for immediately. The family certainly had enough influence to make that happen. If she could put her own mind at ease, Eliza would also be free from anxiety.

⟨⎯⎯⎯⎯⟩

The next few days were hectic. There was so much to pack and instructions to give so the estate would continue to run smoothly while she was gone. Her father would escort them to Falsbury and return the following week. She was glad to have him along. He was more comfort than he realized and very good company. Seated at a small table in the library, Grace went over her final notes. A light breeze rippled the pale blue draperies, distracting her with the soft but crisp sound of silk against taffeta. With a sigh, she took in the vivid purples, pinks, and reds of the lilies, carnations, and lobelia that vied for attention in the garden.

The terrible twist in her gut, her terror of childbirth, had dissipated. Perhaps it would all work out. Women lost husbands, women had babies, life went on. As long as she was not one of those women.

Sammy burst through the door, a paper clenched in his chubby little fist. His cheeks were pink, complementing his red waistcoat. Such a little gentleman...until he opened his mouth.

"I have the list," he said in his loud but practiced grown-up voice. She nodded to let him know she had heard and dipped the point into the inkpot to finish her instructions.

"G-R-A-C-I-E, I H-A-V-E THE L-I-S-T!"

She cringed, hands clamping over her ears. "Samuel Beaumont, did you see me acknowledge you?"

With a grin, he nodded.

"Then why did you scream?"

"You weren't looking at me," he said indignantly.

"I don't need my eyes to hear you, young man. It is improper to raise your voice in front of a woman," she lectured, pointing the quill at him. "Apologize."

"But you're not a woman, you're my sister."

"I am still a female so you will practice your manners on me." She leaned back in the chair, knowing this would not happen in a snap. He had inherited their mother's argumentative nature.

"But Papa says when a man comes to you with an important matter, he should get your full attention. So you have to look at me." Samuel stood straight, shoulders back, as if waiting for his own apology.

"That is not the way to go about it. You should wait patiently until I lift my head."

He stuck out his bottom lip. "I'm sorry if you thought my patience was too loud."

Well, Grace supposed that would have to do. She held out her arms, and he ran into them. Wiggling onto her lap, he tried to smooth the crumpled parchment on the table. "I think I have everything. Read it."

"Why don't you read it for me?"

"I've done enough work this morning. My head hurts from all the thinking." Sammy snuggled back against his sister's chest. She kissed him on top of the head, and gave him a squeeze.

"Fine. Shall we get some breakfast now?" He nodded and ran from the room before she could blink. Looking at his list, she giggled.

THOR
RUG FOR THOR
MY TOEE THEEUTER
ALL MY MARBELS
MY WRLEEGIG
MY PONEE AND CART
MY DOMINOZ

Samuel dashed back into the room. "Can you put my table ninepins on there for me, please? That one was too hard. It made my brain swell." And he was gone again.

"Whoa, slow down," her father said from the hall. He poked his head inside the door. "What are you laughing at?"

"Your son and my brother. I fear he is growing into a manipulative young man. He's already learned how to charm the staff and is working on me."

"He gets that from his mother. I don't have a charming bone in my body," he said in his own defense. "She'd be demmed proud of him, wouldn't she?"

Grace smiled in agreement. "Exceedingly proud."

The sun glinted off the steel spokes of the carriage wheels, a fine breeze stirring the leaves. The driver, four in hand, clicked to the shining chestnut horses and they nickered in anticipation. It would be a three-day journey by coach. She watched Papa sit his massive bay gelding, straight and tall and handsome. Many men his age had gone to fat or lost their hair. Not Lord Boldon. He was as fit as most men half his age. If she married, would she find a man who compared to her father? Highly doubtful.

"Samuel! Step lively, boy! We have new lands to discover!" he shouted out to his son. "Grace, if you give another instruction, we will leave you behind. The place will not fall to the ground without you."

"Look who's so eager to be away." She laughed as the coachman waited for her, his blue uniform matching the red and blue Boldon crest on the door. She settled onto the cushioned velvet seat. "Sammy, I have fresh biscuits with strawberry jam from Mrs. Woolley in case you get hungry. Are you riding with me or with Papa?"

"Papa, can I ride on the big horse?"

"Certainly." Sammy placed his small hand on his father's sturdy forearm. "On the count of three: one, two thr-eee!" The boy jumped with all his strength while Lord Boldon pulled him up. He grabbed his father's coat with his free hand and easily swung up behind him.

"Hail, Caesar!" cried Sammy.

"What?" his father asked "Caesar?"

"Mr. Chenwick yelled it one day. I forgot why he was so excited, but you know how he gets about his history. I remember that part, though."

"Well, I suppose that's a start. Any other little tidbits you remember from your lessons? Entertain me, Samuel. I pay the man enough."

"Well, he was talking to Mrs. Woolley yesterday with a silly smile on his face. All of a sudden, she put her hands on her hips, made a huffing noise, and marched out of the room. Poor Mr. Chenwick looked very confused then decided we would read poetry."

"Which poet did he choose?"

"The Roman, Virgil. He said, 'A woman is an ever pickle and changeable thing.' And then he shook his head and told me never to fall in love."

Lord Boldon let out a belly laugh that Mrs. Woolley, obviously the pickle in the statement, might have heard in the kitchen.

"Selfishness must always be forgiven you know, because there is no hope of a cure."

Jane Austen, *Mansfield Park*

Chapter Six

London
Late June 1815

Carson's refuge was an unassuming brick front on Bedford Place, the outskirts of respectable London. A modest and discreet location lined with residences that housed expensive mistresses. A well-bred woman would never be seen in this neighborhood, and an aristocratic husband would never be noticed. Kit eyed the gold "W" above the entrance before sharply rapping a large brass knocker. A butler, in impeccable dress, opened the door.

"May I help you, sir?" Kit handed him the card he'd received from Lord Coventry. "Yes, my lord. They are expecting you. Follow me, please."

Handing off his hat, Kit followed the man down a darkened hall to a large comfortable room. Polished oak woodwork brightened the décor of dark leather furniture and deep brown and russet wallpaper and rugs. Cold meats, cheeses, and breads were arranged on a side table, next to a selection of Madeira, claret, scotch, brandy, and the finest ale. Several men stood near the window, a few more near the fireplace, and the rest scattered on chairs or sofas. They all turned at once.

Lord Coventry came forward. "Ah, my lord, so good of you to come. Gentlemen, this is Carson's brother, the new Earl of Sunderland."

Bows and murmurs of welcome, and then Weston appeared in front of him, arms wide. They gripped each other, foregoing social protocol. "By Christ, it's good to see you, Kit. You look old, my friend."

"You're no Johnny Raw yourself." He thumped his childhood companion on the back. "It's been too long, Edward." The rest of the earls introduced themselves and eventually all found a seat.

"We have gathered this evening to honor Sunderland in our own way. Carson was a good man, a bang-up cove." Lord Coventry raised his glass.

"Aye, he was."

"Here, here!"

"None better."

Kit heard the responses and grinned. Carson had made his mark with these men. And as the evening went on, each shared a memory. Some tales were adventurous, others sentimental, and one downright comical.

Kit learned a few things about his brother that night. That in itself made it worth the trip. He also made lasting friendships with some interesting fellows.

Lord Coventry began a tale that involved Carson, a bet, a pedestrian curricle, and three Beau

Monde females on Piccadilly Street. "The bacon-brained oaf thought—what the devil was his name? Since he couldn't outrace your brother on a horse, he'd try a different mode of transportation. There was Sunderland, perched on this ridiculously small seat, gripping the handbar white-knuckled, and pushing off with both feet. They're both tottering this way and that, neck and neck, kicking at the ground with their heels to push forward. Neither kept an eye to what lay ahead as they approached Hatchard's bookstore."

"I tried to warn them, but they were both so preoccupied with who was in the lead and keeping their balance," offered Weston, shaking his head in mock despair. "They never saw what hit them."

"But Lady Jersey did. That scream will forever be in my nightmares." Coventry covered both ears with his hands. "Good god, that woman has a voice that could shatter glass."

"Poor Lady Sefton, carrying her bandbox one minute, on her backside the next. And the other fool, clipping the bandbox with one wheel, flattened her new hat." Weston wrapped his arms around his middle, laughing and attempting to catch his breath. "I swear Lady Jersey turned a perfect shade of purple."

"My brother ran over one of Almack's patronesses?" A chuckle began low in Kit's belly, and soon he joined the others in their raucous mirth.

"He bent the frame getting off the bloody thing, then slipped in the mud. When he attempted to sit up," Coventry finished with a flourish, "Lady Cowper said in the calmest voice, 'Why Lord Sunderland, how very gallant of you. I was hesitant to dirty my new slippers.' Then she used his waistcoast to step across the puddle and continued across the street."

With a straight face, Weston added, "Of course, we acted as if we'd never met the dimwit."

Kit's stomach ached. He gulped air and reached for his scotch. Yes, he had come to the right place. Carson would have considered this a fitting send off. This brotherhood preferred to celebrate his life rather than mourn his death. He looked down at the black breeches and waistcoat he would be wearing for the next few months. It seemed such a color day after day was more a penance than a memorial, but he did not make the rules.

"Gentlemen, it's been a pleasure, but I must go home to my wife," said Lord Sussex. "I will say it was an odd experience, having to knock at this establishment's door rather than use my key."

"You have keys?" Kit was intrigued. "To come and go as you please?"

"When you become a member of the Wicked Earls' Club, you are given a key. This is a place you can indulge your vices without worry of discovery. It may be monetary, sexual, or just indulgent," explained Coventry. "It may *not* be unscrupulous, criminal, or physically harmful to anyone in my employ or under my protection. And *all* of my members are under my protection."

"So why did you give it up?" Kit asked Sussex. "You don't seem the type to drop this type of membership on a whim."

"Unfortunately, marriage is the one vice that is not permitted inside these walls. Once you're a tenant for life, the membership is revoked." The earl shrugged. "This was a special evening. Besides, my Tabbie is more than worth it. These rakes don't keep my bed warm at night the way she does." Groans of protest followed his statement, but all the men smiled.

Crystal sifters of cognac appeared on the table. Kit swirled the amber liquid in his glass then sipped. "By god, this is the best stuff I've ever had. Where'd you get it?"

"My secret," replied Conventry.

"One of many," agreed Weston.

At the end of the evening, Weston and Kit flagged a hackney cab and went back to Kit's townhouse. They sipped more port, played some billiards, and Edward told him the latest news of his family.

"What about you? What are your immediate plans?" Weston sat near the table, his long legs stretched out and crossed at the ankles, his hands cupping the back of his dark head. He watched as Kit took aim and sent a ball spiraling into a corner pocket. "And what will Lady Eliza do now?"

"Interesting you should ask." He set his stick down, took a sip of his drink, and leaned on the table. "She's carrying Carson's child."

Edward gave the expected cough and sputter. He waited for the interrogation.

"When did she tell you? Is she sure?" Weston paused. "No, she doesn't need the money. I'm sure between her father and the marriage contract—"

"She doesn't have an ounce of guile in her. My mother has become very attached to her." He sighed. "It just puts me...stranded, so to speak."

"You are the earl unless she has a boy. So, you claim the title for at least seven or eight months?" Weston gave a whistle. "Ain't that a lark."

"I'm conflicted, to tell you the truth. After Waterloo, I swore I was done with war. Yet, a week at home and I miss the army—my regiment, my men. If she had a boy, I could go back to my old life."

"Then let's toast to a boy." Edward held up his glass.

"My mother takes solace from Lady Eliza. My father has taken this hard and looks like hell. I'm worried about him. He's not quite right, but I can't put my finger on it. I'm afraid I may have to assume guardianship of the child."

"It's to be expected, Kit. Not only did he lose a son but his heir. Funny how life can change in the snap of a finger."

Both men were quiet, lost in their thoughts. Kit wondered again about the relationship between his brother and his wife.

"Did he come to love her?"

Weston shook his head. "It was odd. At first, he claimed he was imprisoned, leg-shackled, lost his freedom. Yet he gave up his mistress, went home most nights, and never spoke ill against her. After awhile, when he mentioned her name, I could hear a note of tenderness."

"She insisted on remaining with us after the church service. Lady Eliza appears to be meek and fragile, but there's a stubbornness in her that impressed me." He also respected her loyalty. "I believe she loved Carson."

"He said the same. I think it frightened him, having another person depend on him. Love him like that without demanding anything in return. He had his demons, but I think she was the reason he wanted to change." Edward shrugged. "At the very least, he had come to care for her."

"What makes you say that?"

"His last night, he told me being married pleased him, and he was certain they would be blessed with a healthy child soon."

"All men want heirs."

"Men only wanting an heir say just that. They lament and bemoan the lack of a son, not utter the words 'blessed' and 'child'." Weston raised his eyebrows in challenge.

"Good point." Kit picked up the billiard cue again. "I hope you're right. It would ease my soul to know he was happy at the end."

"I can say with absolute confidence that he was content. That's as close to happiness as most people get, especially a man like Carson. But that comment makes more sense now. I almost asked him what he meant but then the gaming began..."

"Is it true he was foxed?"

Weston nodded. "He really did try to stop. Hadn't had a drink in weeks before that night. You know Carson, once he got started, he couldn't quit. But I've seen him drunker than a wheelbarrow and ride a horse better than me. It was just bloody rotten luck the beast stumbled."

For all of us, thought Kit. The clack of ivory against ivory echoed in the room as Kit cleared the table and held out his hand.

Weston groaned as he gave up the guinea. "It's good to know some things remain constant. Don't think you've ever lost at billiards. Next time, it's a game of hazard."

"If you don't mind a wait. It'll be some time before I can go to any clubs or gaming-hells." Kit wasn't big on either, but he did enjoy good company. Like tonight.

"I'm recommending you as a member of the Earls' Club. Polite society will never know if you sneak out on occasion and lose a few piles to your old friend, Edward." He put a hand on Kit's shoulder. "Consider us your regiment. We recognize past and present members by the pin. If you're ever in a spot, look for one of these." He touched the "W" on his cravat.

"I appreciate that. Believe it or not, I'm happy to be home but frustrated." He gave a slight growl. "I'm a military man, a man of action. Sitting out and waiting for an outcome is about the worst weapon I can face."

"Not to be selfish, *Uncle* Christopher, but I hope it's a girl. I don't want to wait twenty years to have a drink with the next Earl of Sunderland."

"Hmph. Get used to calling *me* Sunderland first. Then we'll worry about infants."

Kit went to bed, his eyes tired but his mind spinning. He hated indecisiveness, didn't hesitate when faced with choices. Yet, he didn't know his own mind when it came to this possible inheritance. He had never believed in fate or destiny but it was definitely giving him a basting now.

"It is not time or opportunity that is to determine intimacy;—it is disposition alone. Seven years would be insufficient to make some people acquainted with each other, and seven days are more than enough for others."

Jane Austen, *Sense and Sensibility*

Chapter Seven

Early July, 1815
Near Falsbury Castle

Sammy moved his finger across the dusty slats of the window, forming the vague image of a bird. It had been a long trip, a few of the roads bone rattling, though much of the bouncing could be attributed to her brother. Grace watched his young, smooth face as he concentrated, his tongue sticking out from the corner of his mouth. When he finished, he turned to her with a bright smile. "I did better with the wings this time, didn't I? They still don't look like the sketch in the book."

Grace studied the half dozen birds adorning the walls of the coach. The wings had begun as triangles, but the most recent attempts looked more like an oval that had been hacked repeatedly with an ax.

"Practice makes perfect. But in my humble opinion, I do believe they could almost take flight."

He peered into her face, holding her gaze. "You aren't just saying that because you're my sister?"

"Heavens no. I swear"—she held up her hand—"it is the finest depiction of a bird I have ever seen grace this carriage. I can't imagine what you'll accomplish by the time you are seven."

"I've been practicing," he agreed smugly. "I'll show you my dogs next. I'm still working on the tails though. They're either too long or too short."

"Whoa, whoa," called the driver to the four chestnut horses. The jingle and clink of rein and bridle was followed by Samuel hanging out the door.

"Sit down right now! It hasn't even stopped yet." She pulled the cord and peered through the window slits.

"I want to know what's happening. I don't see any houses, so something must be wrong." His eyes widened. "Maybe we're being set upon by thieves. And Thor is tied up on top. Oh no!" He slapped his forehead and sank dramatically into the dusty velvet.

"I think three days is all you can handle for one journey. It's broad daylight, you goose. No one robs a coach in the morning. They would at least wait until afternoon." But she was curious as to why they had stopped.

Opening the door again, her brother jumped out. "But it's almost afternoon!"

Papa let out a cheery hallo to someone, and then the low murmur of male voices mixed with the snort of horses and stomp of hooves. She brushed off her blue print skirt, tied her matching bonnet on her head, and stepped out into the bright daylight. Her feet sank into the summer grass and the scent of lavender hung lightly in the air. They had just emerged from a patch of woods, and the brightness caused her eyes to water. As she blinked, a shape formed. A tall, dark figure. She blinked again to clear her vision and drew in a breath. Gracious!

The man rode a huge black beast that pranced and threw its head as the pair approached their party. He wore buckskins stretched across muscled thighs, and his boots were dull from travel. Her eyes moved up to the strong hands that held the reins with ease. He had foregone gloves, and pushed up his sleeves, revealing the powerful forearms beneath. With a slight tug and a click of his tongue, the horse obediently settled down and dropped its head.

"Good day, my lady." Her stomach fluttered at the deep timbre and her fingertips fiddled with her skirt. The voice sounded oddly familiar but...

"Look who we've stumbled upon," said her father, trotting up on his big bay. "I wager we're heading to the same place."

Grace held her hand over her eyes and squinted. Her heart was racing, and she wanted to *shoosh* the roar in her ears. Christopher Roker. The twin she had danced with and thought about for weeks afterward. He turned his eyes on her, and the late morning rays set fire to her face. Oh, why did her legs feel as limp as Mrs. Woolley's curls after a rain? And why did this man affect her so?

"Lady Grace, I hope you are well. I understand you're to spend some time at Falsbury." He gave a half bow from his horse, his shoulders straining the white linen shirt. His dark coat had been discarded, rolled up, and tied behind his saddle. His black waistcoat emphasized his tanned skin. The man was ruggedly attractive. An unbidden smile crept onto her lips.

"Good day, Lord...Sunderland. I'm looking forward to our visit." She wondered if it upset him to be addressed by his brother's title so soon. "Are we close, then?"

"Very close," answered Lord Sunderland. "May I show you?"

He swung his leg over the saddle and dropped to the ground. Grace looked away from his backside, her breath caught in her throat. Sammy tugged at her skirt, but she swatted at his hand. "Gracie, who is he?" he whispered loudly. "He doesn't look like a highwayman."

"No, I'm afraid I'm just a poor soldier finding his way home," answered the earl. "And you are?"

"Sammy. I mean..." He put his shoulders back and with a perfect bow, he announced in a regal tone, "Samuel, Viscount of Tyne at your service."

Grace pressed her lips together to hold in the giggle. Her little brother would be mortified if she laughed at him now. *Thank you, my sweet Sammy, for bringing me back to earth,* she thought. With a lungful of air and a hand on her stomach to hold in those pesky wings, she turned to face the handsome man in front of her.

"Well, I am in good company. Would you like to see my favorite view of the castle before we continue?"

Lord Boldon dismounted and came forward with a bow. "It's good of you to have us. I must say, I didn't know if it was good idea for my daughter to visit at this time. But both she and Eliza were insistent. I hope it doesn't put anyone out."

The earl shook his head then glanced over his shoulder at Grace, his dark eyes narrowed. The sun glinted off his raven hair, damp wisps curling over his stiff collar. His shirt, not quite closed, revealed the glisten of sweat across his broad chest.

She licked her lips.

He smiled.

Ebony eyes raked over her and sent another wave of heat up her neck. A new sensation stirred low in her belly and her hand hovered protectively over it. Stepping forward, he bowed once more. "I hoped we would meet again. I am happy to give you the first glimpse of my childhood home."

He held out his arm. Grace looked to her father, who nodded his head, and she laid her fingers on the earl's sleeve. *Breathe, you dimwit, breathe. He's just a man,* she told herself. *Just a perfect specimen of a man.*

The three of them walked to the top of a hill. The trees showed bright green and silver, the wind whistling above their heads. The fresh air was a relief after the stagnant coach.

"Where is your sword, if you are a soldier?"

"Fortunately, we've run the enemy off for now so I can take a bit of a holiday. It's very heavy, you know." He winked at Grace.

"I hope I'm as good at fighting as I am at sketching." Sammy ran in front—then in back—then in front of them again. "Oh, Gracie, you'll like this," he yelled when he reached the top of the hill.

Below them stood a magnificent building, at least three times the size of Boldon. Four round towers stood sentry on each corner of the enormous structure, a flag flying from each. Between the towers, four stories of windows glittered against the silver stone. Arrow slits, carved from the top of the walls, stirred her imagination. Centuries ago, a group of knights would have cantered up the slope, their banners gently wafting the royal and family crests. Falsbury Castle rose steadfastly over a lush emerald valley, its shadow almost swallowing the small village below. Crushed stone formed the sizeable rectangular drive in front of the building; tiny bodies moved around like ants. Dots of color, most likely large pots of geraniums, added color to the scene. Grace sighed in delight.

"Splendid, isn't it?" Sunderland asked quietly.

A shrill whistle startled her. Sammy grinned up at them. "You're a king and a soldier?" he asked.

She heard the rumble of Sunderland's chuckle as he tousled the boy's hair. "Far from it. I did imagine myself a Templar knight when I was a boy. My brother and I would climb to the battlement and have sword fights."

"Let's go! Let's go! I want to climb to the top of the palace." Sammy spun around and went down the hill, his hair shining gold in the afternoon sun.

"I must say, it is an impressive sight, like something from a fairy tale," her father agreed. He pointed to a small lake to the right of the castle grounds. A graceful willow bowed over the water. "Do you keep it stocked?"

"Of course, bream is my father's favorite. The cook likes plenty of roach, and there's pike. They always put up a good fight."

"Indeed. Almost as good as trout."

The beauty surrounding them was stunning. Grace peeked at Lord Sunderland's profile. This was a perfect background for him. She turned to see her father looking at her with an odd expression in his eyes. It made her uncomfortable, as if he knew what was going through her mind. Sammy yelled again, and they returned at a leisurely pace. This time, she took Papa's arm to better maintain her composure.

His muscles tensed as he watched the sway of her hips. She was lovely. Bright chestnut curls peeked out from the bonnet, swirling against her alabaster skin. He wanted to reach out and touch one of those soft locks, feel the smoothness of her cheek against his finger. The traveling dress fluttered in the breeze, the thin material caressing long, shapely legs. He imagined those burnished red curls falling down her back.

When Kit met her at the wedding, he'd been attracted by her beauty and the vivacity in her clear green eyes. As they danced, he had enjoyed her intelligence and wit. But seeing her here in his favorite spot—catching her off guard and so approachable, he wanted to gather her in his arms and kiss her. He and Carson had lain on this grassy slope for hours as children, dreaming of knights and battles and rescued maidens. Looking at her face as she took in the castle grounds, Kit swore she had the same images in her head.

Ridiculous. But when she licked those plump lips...

Good god man, he thought. *Mind your manners or find yourself a willing kitchen wench.* He needed a diversion before he made a fool of himself. The emotion of the past few weeks must be getting to him.

"Papa, I need to get my toy chest down. I have to show Lord Sunderland my sword."

"Wait until we get unpacked. Our host may have business matters to deal with. Do not intrude upon his time." Lord Boldon shook his finger for emphasis.

Kit liked the boy. Samuel was just the distraction he needed and would bring some much-needed joy back into those cold, damp halls.

"Do you ride much, Lord Tyne?" he asked Samuel as the driver helped Lady Grace back into the coach.

"Yes, very well my father says," he announced proudly. "Do you?"

"I believe I'm adequate," he admitted with a solemn nod. "Would you like to ride with me the rest of the way? I've been traveling alone since London and would appreciate the company."

Sammy looked at his father, his eyes pleading.

"If you promise to behave and not wiggle too much." Lord Boldon looked again at Sunderland. "Are you sure? You can drop him to the ground any time you've had enough. He'd still arrive before us."

Kit laughed. "I think we'll be fast friends."

"And remember your manners in conversation. Give Lord Sunderland time to answer before you move on to another subject," Grace added through one of the slits of the window.

She held his gaze for a moment then the slats snapped shut. An innocent, to be sure. He'd realized that when he danced with her. Today, she had taken in his appearance with wide eyes. He recognized the appreciative gaze, had seen it enough times in his bachelor life. The pink in her cheeks and the sudden aversion of her eyes told him she was naïve in the ways of seduction. An experienced flirt would not have gaped so openly or looked away with such haste. She would reveal more in the coming weeks. For now, the castle was calling him.

He rolled his stiff shoulders and neck to ease the soreness from a long day travel. It was time to trade the saddle in for a brandy and a bath. Then he would enjoy his Italian wet and dry sweetmeats at supper tonight. His mouth watered. Their old cook, Mrs. Whitten, was an angel in the kitchen.

His leg jiggled. Kit looked down to see Samuel pulling on his stirrup irons with the same urgency he had tugged on his sister's skirt. "Papa says I'm big enough to ride pillion instead of in front."

"I agree. You look strong, but we'll see if your arms are long enough."

Lord Boldon swung Samuel onto the back of the horse. The boy stretched his arms around Kit's waist as far as possible then clutched the hem of his waistcoat. "Hold on, now. And tell me if I need to slow down," Kit instructed as the boy settled into a comfortable position.

"I like to go fast. My legs are strong too. I can hold on tight, I promise."

As the party ambled down the road, Samuel kept up a stream of one-sided conversation. The familiar landscape brought back so many memories to Kit. He and Carson hiding out in the woods, eating the cherry pie they'd stolen from the kitchen. They had raced up and down this hill on their ponies. Carson always kicked his so furiously to win that the pony had bucked him off once. Kit had laughed so hard he too had fallen on his backside. The brook below gurgled and sparkled, where they had fished with bamboo poles and concocted daring adventures. *I feel you here, brother. I'm glad I came back,* he thought. This was where he could mend his body, heal his heart. Death, in battle and at home, had drained the life from him. He needed to replenish his faith in mankind and restore the optimism that had always kept him balanced.

Kit suppressed a smile as the youngster provided a steady stream of interesting tidbits. Lord Boldon liked to sit in front of the fire every night with his port and remember Mama. In the mornings, he washed with very cold water to *invinegar* himself and yelled like a banshee. Mrs. Woolley always had a silly look on her face when she brought tea or a repast for his tutor. But when Mr. Chenwick smiled at her, she would scowl at him and pretend she didn't like him. Girls were strange and contrary. They would cry when they were happy.

Excellent trout were stocked in the lake at Boldon, he informed Kit as he dashed from one subject to another in the same breath. Samuel's favorite lure was a green and white silk minnow with feathers for the tail and fins. His father preferred lobworms, and they tricked Gracie once and he pretended to eat one. His sister was also like his mother because Lady Boldon had died when he was born. But Papa and Gracie told him everything about Mama and kept pictures of her so she would live on in their hearts until they were all reunited.

And no, Gracie didn't care for any man except Papa, who said she would be a spinster if he didn't get her to London and find her a husband.

"Your sister is looking for a husband?" Perhaps he should keep his distance. A wife remained optional for him if an heir was born in December. He had written his commander and explained the situation, hoping to be back in uniform the following year.

"No, that's what makes Papa grumble. She says she has no use for another man. Her hands are full with the two she already has. That's us," Samuel explained, poking his thumb at his chest.

"Indeed. I'm sure you keep your sister busy."

The boy grinned. "I do my best."

"I must say, Lord Tyne, we've become fast friends on this ride." He chuckled, imagining the horror in Lady Grace's forest green eyes if she'd heard their conversation. She may be a safe diversion after all. Nothing wrong with a little harmless flirtation with a beautiful woman, who seemed willing enough.

"You can call me Sammy. Oh, Papa made me promise not to do all the talking. What's your favorite thing to do?"

"Listen to young men divulge their family secrets." He grinned and clucked to the horse. Yes, it was good to be home.

*"Friendship is certainly the finest balm for
the pangs of disappointed love."*

Jane Austen, *Northanger Abbey*

Chapter Eight

Whoa, whoa there." The stone crunched under
the steel rims. The horses slowed to a stop, and
the driver clambered down. Several servants
emerged from the front entrance, including the
butler. The carriage door opened, and she rose from
the cushioned seat. Bending her head, her hand
outstretched, she stepped from the carriage. But her
fingers grazed warm skin, not the coachman's gloved
hand. She found herself face-to-face again with Lord
Sunderland. When his face slanted in a smile
beneath those glittering black eyes, her heart
trembled. It was hard to believe there had been two
men on this earth so handsome.

"Can I get my sword now? Please?"

Grace, glad to attend to something besides her
thoughts of Lord Sunderland, shook her head and
turned to the coachman. "Would you remove Master
Samuel's traveling cases down first? His sword
seems to be of the utmost importance."

"Yes, my lady." The ropes were tugged and
untied and soon the gravel beside the coach was

littered with luggage. Servants began lugging the cases inside, leather thumping against the stone steps as they strained with the weight.

Grace heard her cousin first. "Gr-a-c-ie!" She burst through the doorway, paused as she searched the crowd, and locked eyes with her cousin. "Gracie, oh Gracie!" Eliza rushed down the steps and across the drive, her dress clinging to the slight rise of her belly. They hugged as if it had been years. Both women laughed, wiped away tears, and babbled to each other at the same time.

"Sammy, I believe we will fend for ourselves this afternoon." Sunderland grinned at Lord Boldon. "Would you mind if I made him my squire for the day?"

"I couldn't think of a better activity for him after three days in a coach. In fact, I'd be happy to tag along after I've washed off the dust."

"Find your sword, boy. We'll stop in the kitchen, clean up a bit, and see what Mrs. Whitten has to sustain a knight in training. I will teach you the art of battle before supper."

Sammy tore through his trunk and produced his wooden sword. He ran to Eliza. "Aren't you glad we came?" he asked. Not waiting for an answer, the boy hugged Grace, bowed to his father, and took the earl by the hand. "Let's go! Let's go! Papa, we have to find you a weapon."

"I'll see you on the battlement, son."

They disappeared through the entrance and quiet assailed the group. "Phew! He gets more energetic with each passing year," remarked Eliza as she turned to kiss her uncle on both cheeks. "Oh, my lord. It is so good to see you. Thank you for bringing Gracie to me."

"I shudder to think what might have happened if I'd refused." He patted her on the shoulder. "I do hope all goes well for you." His eyes drifted to her middle.

Eliza's hand rubbed her stomach. "Oh, yes. And Lady Falsbury has been wonderful. She's arranging a light repast for us. We shall meet up with her after you've settled into your rooms."

The two girls chatted as they strolled arm in arm, oblivious to the bustle going on around them. The horses were led away, one shying at the snapping banners overhead. Grace thought the outside was imposing but stopped once inside, her mouth falling open. "Goodness."

Her cousin laughed as Grace took in the huge entry. "Intimidating, isn't it?" The stone was covered on each side with life-sized portraits. The past marquesses of Falsbury studied them with practiced disinterest. A variety of medieval weapons graced the walls before them. Next to a staircase, a suit of armor stood sentry, holding a battle-ax.

"Let's get you settled in your rooms so you can freshen up," declared Eliza. "Then we'll join Lady Falsbury."

The open circular staircase had been added over the centuries. They followed several servants, carrying boxes and chests of clothes, up the marble steps. Grace noted her cousin leaned heavily on the handrail. Advancing to the first floor, Eliza stopped halfway down the hall. "Uncle, your room is two more doors over. We provided Grace and Samuel with connecting rooms. I knew she would want to keep an eye on him."

The chamber was large and covered in lilac paper with a repeating pattern of tiny white and pink flowers. The bed curtains were pulled back from the four-poster bed, a canopy of pale purple gracing the top. A summer board, painted with a vase of greenery and flowers, covered the opening to the fireplace. Eliza sat down on the mattress, wiping her forehead.

"You must be ready for a bath, cousin. It is so warm today. I don't know how you managed inside the coach. It must have been stifling."

"It was heat or a layer of dust over me. It's bad enough with the slats barely cracked, but leave them wide open and I'd look like a field hand. I didn't know if Lady Falsbury would greet us or not, and I certainly wasn't taking a chance that she'd see me like that."

"You seem to have made an impression on Kit."

"Kit?"

"Lord Sunderland. Due to our...past, he decided if we were not in public, I could use his given name—Kit or Christopher. In time, he said, we will all be used to his title."

"And why would you say I impressed him? We hardly spoke when we met on the road." She silently cursed the heat rising up her neck again. "He showed us his favorite view of the castle."

"Now I know he was impressed. That was a very special place for him and Carson." Her eyes narrowed as she studied Grace. "You're colouring up."

"No, I'm just—just warm."

"This is me, so stop with the excuses. Something is going on. When I looked out the window, I saw Kit dismount and almost run to the carriage to help you out."

"I'm sure he was just being gracious."

"He's a soldier. His manners may need a bit of polishing, but I'll pursue this conversation later. After I've observed both of you more." Her eyes glistened as she added, "Thank you so much for coming. I knew nothing would keep you away."

"You look weary, Eliza. Are you ill?" Grace hadn't meant to blurt out her concerns but she'd had too much time while they travelled to think about the dangers of childbirth.

"No, I tire easily but haven't been sick at all. That was one reason it took me some time to figure out I was with child. But after I missed my second menses, I told Carson."

Grace pulled off her bonnet and plunked down next to Eliza. Her bottom sank into the soft down of the top mattress, and she leaned back, spreading her arms above her head.

"Oh, this is heaven. The last inn we stayed at only had four ticks on the bedframe and the top mattress was filled with chaff. Better than straw, mind you, but I missed my feathers and smooth linen sheets."

"Lady Falsbury insists on the best of everything. You will be quite spoiled before you leave." Eliza stretched out next to her cousin, her elbow sinking into the soft stuffing, and propped her head on her palm. "Oh, I could take a nap."

"I'll understand if you do. But first, could you arrange for a lady's maid for me? I had to leave mine behind. Her sister was getting married, and I didn't have the heart to make her miss the wedding."

"That's just like you. I'll talk to Lady Falsbury. And I couldn't possibly sleep when you've just arrived. We have so much to talk about." Pain flashed across her violet eyes. She stared up at the canopy. "It was dreadful, Gracie, and then his brother came home. The first time I saw Kit again, I almost collapsed. It was hard to come to terms with Carson's death when his mirror image greets you at breakfast."

"Oh my, I can't imagine."

"It's easier now that I've come to know Kit. They really were nothing alike." Eliza shrugged. "Sometimes I wake up and have to remember all over again that Carson is gone."

"You loved him, didn't you?"

"I worshipped him. He was the first kind man I knew besides your papa. Father barely allowed Mama to introduce me to society before he agreed to the marriage contract. It was all done so quickly. I'd only met him a few times when the banns were called. I expected to be used as a broodmare and then ignored. He didn't seem to care about me one way or the other before the wedding."

"But he did care?" Grace's heart broke for this lovely young woman who deserved so much more than a brief encounter with love.

She shook her head. "Our wedding night was...gentle. I think he understood my fear, almost as if he knew about my father, and said he would never strike me and would always treat me with respect. He touched me as if I were a fragile doll."

Grace remembered the conversation she'd had with Lord Chris—Sunderland. Was her uncle's reputation so widely known? "He was kind and considerate, then?"

A shy smile curled Eliza's lips. "Oh yes. Gracie, it was the most wonderful thing. I had no idea a union between a man and a woman could be so pleasurable. You wouldn't be frightened of marriage if you knew how it could be."

"I'm not frightened of marriage. My parents had a wonderful relationship full of love and respect. I just don't want to *be* married. There is a difference." She knew her tone was defensive and saw the hurt in Eliza's eyes.

"Oh, please don't be angry. I didn't mean to offend you."

Grace sat up and pulled her cousin with her. "You are my best friend in the world. I'm just a bit irritable from the trip. Tell me more about you and Carson."

Eliza's face softened. "He was charming and had a great sense of humor. He teased me but was never cruel. I know I was a dolt, always looking at him with cow eyes."

"You were happy?"

"So happy that I thought my luck had finally turned. Carson began to bring me little treats. He said he liked to see me smile, that he'd never met a person who possessed my true sincerity."

"He did come to know you then." Grace squeezed her cousin's hand, now taking comfort in the fact she had known love before her husband died.

Eliza took a breath and continued, "The first time he brought me a posy, I cried. I was such a muttonhead. It took me by surprise. He was like a little boy, almost shy, afraid I might laugh at him or turn my nose up at the flowers. Instead, I was a dimwit and burst into tears. When he took my face in his palms and looked into my eyes... I saw it."

"Saw what?"

"The affection he held for me. He was beginning to care for me." She stopped for a moment, rubbing her belly in slow, wide circles. "When he took me that night, it was different. He didn't touch me as if I would break. He was tender but demanding, and I knew it would happen. I knew he would love me some day." The grief in her eyes slashed through Grace's heart.

"And then he was gone. Gracie, why? Why would God give me someone to love only to take him away? Give me a tiny glimpse of happiness and then snatch it from me?"

"I don't know, Eliza. I don't know." The tears slid down her own face now. "And when you told him you were having his child?"

"He stopped drinking and only went out once or twice a week. The baby was our secret at first. News the two of us could keep to ourselves for a little while before the world intruded upon our blissful state. Those few weeks were perfect."

They sat in silence, both lost in their own thoughts. Grace was thinking of the loss of her mother again, empathy surging inside her knowing Eliza was feeling the same despair and emptiness. Marriage seemed to bring nothing but misery. Husbands that mistreated their wives, couples who did not hold any mutual affection for each other, or death. Why would she want to take such a risk?

"Goodness, look at us," sniffed Eliza, wiping her face with both hands. "You'll order that carriage to take you home if I continue this Friday face." She threw her arms around Grace and hugged her. "From now on, only positive thoughts. Lady Falsbury says that the baby's temperament will take on mine. So I need to keep a cheerful disposition." Her hand went to her belly again. "And I take great solace in this child. A piece of Carson to cherish, as Sammy keeps your mother's memory alive."

"I promise you, we will get through this, and we'll stay as long as you need us. Or until my brother sets up your bristles and you send us away." Grace laughed then kissed her cheek. "Let's find Lady Falsbury and then see if we can track down those errant knights!"

"Always laugh when you can. It is cheap medicine."

Lord Byron

Chapter Nine

Good God! Was the boy finally tiring? No, Kit was exhausted and the boy was indefatigable. And quite good with a wooden sword. Kit had shown the youngster a few basic parries and attacks. He had learned quickly. Too quickly, he thought with chagrin, rubbing the eye he almost lost when Sammy jumped up unexpectedly. To the boy's credit, he began to cry when he thought he'd blinded Kit. That led to another ten minutes of calming the child. He had also learned that sugared almonds were a good distraction for a wailing five-year-old.

After an hour of full-out play, Kit was thinking of his last real battle with relish. Soldiers didn't duck and crawl between the enemy's legs or jump on their shoulders and tickle them under the armpit. It was dirty fighting, and the boy was demmed good at it. He had a new respect for Samuel and bribed him with some marzipan so an old man could catch his breath.

"Lord Sunderland, how goes it?"

Sammy dropped his sword and ran to his father, leaping into his arms without warning. He gave a grunt as he took the force of his son's weight against his solid chest. "Papa, I've been learning to fight like a knight. I'll need armor next. Sunderland says it will protect me from cuts and bruises."

Boldon squinted at the earl. "And perhaps a helmet to protect your eyes, eh?"

"Tell me it's not swelling," Kit asked with a rueful grin, his fingers gingerly pressing around his socket.

The older man pressed his lips together and shrugged. "My eyesight's not what it used to be. Perhaps it's naught but afternoon shadow or the way you are standing."

"It's my fault, Papa. Remember how we practiced being frogs that day by the lake?"

"I remember *you* trying to jump like a frog. And what does that have to do with Sunderland's swollen eye?" He crossed his arms over his chest. "Samuel, no more horseplay! Haven't we discussed this?"

Kit wanted to disappear over the edge of the battlement. A child was being reprimanded for playing too rough—with his adult host, who had fought ten years to earn his fearless reputation in battle. Hand-to-hand combat. The absurdity of it smacked him in the face.

A chuckle turned into a deep rumble that began in his belly and pushed up and out of his throat. By Christ, it made him feel a stone lighter. Sammy cocked his head in question then joined him, followed by his father. The three were holding their guts, doubled over, loud guffaws echoing over the turret. A tear rolled down Kit's cheeks, and he collapsed against the stone wall. Sammy fell onto

Kit's lap, and Boldon leaned over the parapet, wiping at his eyes.

The last time he'd laughed that hard had been with Carson, before he entered the army. His stomach hurt, his eyes burned, his throat was dry, and he hadn't felt this bloody good in years. With a jolt, Kit realized he missed it—the informal camaraderie, these moments of unexpected mirth, and family. The past ten years, his body had been sated with the grimness of war, a somberness of not knowing which of his men would return to their tents, careful not get too attached to anyone under his command. There had been glimpses of forced hilarity—the gaudy humor of soldiers around a campfire, the strained laughter of men knowing this might be their last meal, last joke, last night on this earth. Kit had lost the balance in his life. The careful balance that allowed the mind to accept there was evil in the world but joy still remained: the innocence of a giggling child, the delight of a simple job well done, the tender touch of a beautiful woman...

As the three caught their breath, he had the peculiar feeling they weren't alone. At the top of the stairs, Lady Eliza stood with her mouth gaping, and Lady Grace's eyes danced with amusement though her hand mercifully covered her grin. But her trembling shoulders gave her away. She took in her father and brother, shaking her head as if this were a common occurrence. But when her gaze lingered on him, he detected surprised approval. It was his turn to blush. *Nothing like losing one's dignity right from the start*, he thought. *But blast it, it had been worth every minute.*

"Gracie, I'm a knight and I almost blinded Lord Sunderland with my wicked moves. So then I cried but he gave me sweets and then we fought more until he was so tired I thought *he* might cry. And then Papa came while we were eating marzipan and Papa said something funny... What *did* you say, Papa?"

Lord Boldon pulled himself away from the wall. "It no longer matters." He took a deep breath and wiped at his eyes again. "However, I do believe your training is complete for today. I assume you're collecting this heathen for a good scrubbing and change of clothes?"

"Very intuitive, Uncle. Due to"—Eliza's face clouded briefly—"the lack of entertaining, Lady Falsbury finds the earlier country schedule to her liking. Dinner is served at four-thirty, my lords."

That suited Kit fine. He found himself in his old routine of waking at dawn, and riding or hunting every morning to keep fit. If he returned to his old life, his body would suffer from lack of exercise. He wondered when the family rose at Boldon. City hours or country hours? He bet the latter.

Lady Grace had changed into an olive dress with a black satin ribbon just above her waistline, embroidered in deep green flowers that matched her eyes. The material clung to her curves; the color emphasized that glorious mane of hair. Her bonnet was off and ringlets of copper bounced against her flushed cheeks as she moved forward to take Sammy's hand. She bent over, exposing the tops of her creamy white breasts. His eyes lingered then moved up the slender throat. It begged for a trail of kisses, and he imagined his lips moving along her jawline until he reached her lips.

"Don't you agree, Lord Sunderland?" Grace asked, still bending slightly to hold her brother's hand.

He tore his eyes from her mouth and forced himself to meet her gaze. "I beg your pardon?" He definitely needed to see to his needs if he was going to have a decent conversation with this woman over the next month. Why did the chit always throw him off-balance?

"Rising early in the morning means a productive day." Lady Grace's eyebrows rose; her lips pressed together between her teeth as she tried to maintain a straight face. He'd been caught in his reverie of her...attributes.

"Why, yes. Yes, I've always been an early riser. Nothing like the colors of dawn to take your breath away." Damn, those lips again.

"Hmmph." Lord Boldon cleared his throat, his glance darting between his daughter and his host. "Come, Samuel, I think we'll dress for dinner together. Thank Lord Sunderland for the lesson."

The boy did so with an eloquent bow, and father and son disappeared down the narrow stone steps. Kit stood and brushed himself off, executing his own bow for the ladies. "May I escort you down?"

They both stared at him without a word. Had he not spoken aloud? Then Lady Eliza reached out to touch his eye. "Kit, what happened?"

"Oh, this? It's nothing."

Lady Grace gasped. "Sammy did that, didn't he? When he said he almost blinded you. Oh that naughty boy."

"It is the consequence of male antics. Believe me, I deserved it for underestimating my opponent." He bowed again, thinking to start fresh.

"At least let me tend you. Please, let's go to the kitchen and get a cold compress for the swelling. It's not too terrible yet and we if we treat it right away, I may be able to reduce the bruising." She turned to Lady Eliza. "Do you know if there is any arnica in the kitchen garden or hanging in the still room?"

Her cousin looked at her blankly.

"A surgeon gave some of my men that herb for sea sickness on the short journey to France." Kit wondered where this was leading. "My stomach is fine, I assure you."

"It also helps to reduce bruising in injuries," Lady Grace said brightly. "Come, we'll see what we can find."

And this was how Kit found himself under the command of Captain Grace Beaumont. There was a pleasant authority surrounding her that made others want to do her bidding. With only a few requests, given with efficiency and a kind but firm tone, she had the cook sending staff in four different directions. A young boy returned first with a bucket of cold water from the well. Another young girl returned with witch hazel, which Grace poured into the water.

The smell of rising dough filled the large room. Eliza clasped her stomach, her face pale. "Please excuse me. The pungent scent of the yeast is not agreeing with me for some reason. I think I'll check on Lady Falsbury and see you both at dinner."

"Oh, my poor dear. I thought you hadn't had any sickness?"

"No, but certain odors just turn my insides upside down. There is no reason to what may affect me. So, if you'll excuse me..." And with that, she rushed from the humid room, and Lady Grace returned her attentions to Kit.

"I'll try not to hurt you, but I need to make sure there are no scratches that could become inflamed."

Her fingertips gently pressed at the skin around his eye and pulled his eyelid down. Her breath was warm on his skin and smelled of vanilla and lemon. A wicked thought—tongue stroking hers, and tasting the citrus that filled his nostrils—made him catch his breath.

"I'm so sorry," she said, obviously thinking she had caused him pain.

"I'm fine," he assured her. "I've had much worse in my career."

Satisfied, she laid a cold compress against his left eye and instructed him to tip his head back. She stood to his right, leaning against the massive walnut table in the center of the kitchen. With his head back and his good eye down, Kit had a perfect view of those ivory mounds. A smile curled his lips. This day was improving by the hour.

The cook came back in, out of breath and waving some yellow flowers in her hand. She pushed her frizzy gray hair back under her cap. "Here it is, my lady. Will this be enough?"

"Yes, perfect." The smile of thanks Lady Grace gave Mrs. Whitten had the old woman beaming. Her capable hands diced the arnica with a large knife, only pausing to wipe the sweat off her forehead with a sleeve.

Another servant scurried over from the fireplace with a small pot of boiling water.

"Mrs. Whitten, this needs to be simmered and ground into a paste. Could you do that for me?" Lady Grace asked. "Keep that compress on your eye, my lord. I didn't tell you to remove it yet."

"I'd be happy to," the cook scraped the chopped herb into a pile. Her wrinkled skin belied the youthfulness in her bright eyes as she grinned at her master. "He's not used to *taking* orders, though, as he's always *given* them. Ye'll have to watch that one."

"Well, the boot is quite on the other leg today, isn't it?" Lady Grace removed the cloth from his grip and dipped it into the cold bucket again. "Tell me you will be cooperative, Lord Sunderland, and assuage my guilt in this matter."

"That depends on what you ask of me." Kit enjoyed the look of challenge in her direct gaze. Where had the doe-eyed girl gone from this morning? This woman would be a formidable opponent in anything she set her mind to.

"You will need to apply the salve twice a day, in the evening before you retire and when you rise in the morning."

"Consider me a willing patient." His tone was low, meant only for her ears. "Especially if you apply it for me." The pink creeping up her face made him grin, but her words hid any embarrassment.

"I believe Mrs. Whitten might still box your ears if you act untoward." A mumble of agreement sounded from behind them. "Do not think because of our close quarters, you may act with any kind of familiarity, sir."

He flinched as she applied the fresh compress with unnecessary force. She had certainly put him in his place. But her next words had him grinning again.

"No matter how handsome or charming you may be."

Kit suspected Lady Grace might be the best cure for what ailed him.

"I have been a selfish being all my life, in practice, though not in principle."

Jane Austen, *Pride and Prejudice*

Chapter Ten

Mid July 1815

Grace dressed quickly and smoothed the chemise over her hips. She wrinkled her nose at the corset but slipped it on. With a skilled hand, she reached behind, yanked the ties in the middle, and then pulled the strings at the bottom. Her maid would tighten it properly when she dressed for breakfast. The poor thing had been appalled to learn Grace had dressed herself the first morning. She'd learned to do a passable job around thirteen when she began her early morning forays. With the bodiced petticoat, silk stockings, and garters in place, she donned her pale yellow morning dress. The white lace trim on the neck and sleeves was wearing thin but no one would see her at this hour.

A routine had been established in the last week. As always, Grace rose between six and half past. She would peek in Sammy's room then take the narrow back stairs, wander several hallways, another set of stairs, and find herself in the kitchen. The gardens just beyond were peaceful and smelled heavenly. The fresh morning dew sparkled silver on the leaves, accentuating the yellow, pink, and red petals that were in bloom. She stopped by the herb plot, ran her fingers over the rosemary, and held them to her nose. The pine and lemon scent tickled her nostrils as she looked beyond the gardens to the rolling hills beyond.

Twice this week, she had seen Lord Sunderland on his great black horse, far off in the distance, cantering up a hill or into the woods. His tall form, dark in his mourning coat, stood out against the stark white trunks of the silver birch that mingled with towering oaks. The fact he rose even earlier than she made her smile for some reason. *Though, the man himself seems to have made it his mission to make me smile,* she thought as she absently rubbed the soft green needles again.

"Rosemary is for remembrance,
Between us day and night.
Wishing that I may always,
Have you present in my sight."

Grace's hand froze midway to her nose. Her stomach fluttered as the sultry voice dripped over her. Without turning to face him, she replied with a quick wit,

"And when I cannot have
As I have said before,
Then Cupid, with his deadly dart,
Doth wound my heart full sore."

"Do you often surprise gentlewomen strolling alone in the garden, my lord?" How could she have not felt his approach? His presence was almost overpowering. Her skin prickled, and she resisted the urge to rub her bare arms.

"Only the most beautiful of women, Lady Grace." He stepped in front of her and bowed. "I do apologize if I frightened you. So do you believe in the power of rosemary?"

"For memory? I don't know, but the poem is lovely. A medieval ballad, isn't it?" She looked at him under the cover of her long lashes. So handsome. His eye had healed completely, not even a faint bruise remained. "You don't seem the poetic type, Lord Sunderland."

"My mother taught me that one when I was young. Yes, I do enjoy a well-written line. You might find I'm full of surprises if you get to know me, my lady."

Had he just thrown down a gauntlet? How she loved a challenge. "If you are staying the length of my visit, I will do my best. But for now"—she looked around, realizing they were alone—"I must take my leave before someone thinks we arranged a tryst."

With a bow, he bid her good morning. "I shall see you later today then."

With a brisk stride, Grace hurried up the path. There was no one but their own families present, but servants could be just as bad with gossip. Papa would be mortified if he thought she was alone in the garden with an eligible bachelor. Or he'd turn a blind eye and cross his fingers.

During a game of Loo a few evenings past, her father had asked the earl what his plans were if Eliza had a boy. Sunderland had shrugged. He would return to a military career unless his father needed him. That had led to a discussion of politics, and in turn, Bonaparte and Wellington. Halfway through a discourse of the French rise and ultimate fall,

Sunderland paused and begged pardon from the ladies for the dull conversation.

"Nonsense!" Papa's voice had boomed across the room. "It's only our two families, and I often discuss current events with my daughter. She's quite astute, you know."

The pounding of her heart had echoed through her core as Sunderland regarded her. "I have no doubt," had been his only reply, but his eyes had gleamed with humor.

While the evenings might have been sedate compared to London entertainment, she found herself looking forward to the nightly games in the drawing room. Lady Falsbury was a wicked whist player. Her stoic face never showed her hand until she giggled with glee and took the pot. Eliza played the piano while Grace joined in with lyrics. Sammy would lend his clear, high voice and bow formally afterwards, as if he'd performed on stage. There was no dancing, of course, since the hosts were in mourning. She didn't mind. The company was wonderful and such a change from the usual book or embroidery in front of the fire. By the end of week, Eliza's color had returned, and both women were having a splendid visit.

One evening after dinner, the ladies were enjoying tea. Lady Falsbury and Eliza both had their heads bent over their needlework when the men joined them.

"I must say, when these color patterns first came out, I thought it silly," commented the marchioness. "But the weaker my eyes become, the more I appreciate not squinting to see the color. The headaches it can give one."

"The stitches are very small. I cannot wait to see these tiny boots on the baby." Eliza rubbed her stomach with a contented smile. "My mother is sending me scraps of material from her dresses and scraps of clothing from my childhood to make her a quilt."

"To make *him* a quilt. That will be an excellent project for cooler weather," agreed her mother-in-law.

Grace didn't have the patience for needlework, though she blustered through when necessary. She hated to sit without some type of activity and last night had finished *The Corsair* by Lord Byron. "Papa, would you care to play a game of Spillikins?"

He shook his head and patted his belly. "I fear after such a good dinner and fine port, I'm enjoying a sedentary activity, watching these fine ladies at work."

"A walk around the room, Lady Grace? I also find myself loath to sit," asked Lord Sunderland. He stood and offered his right elbow.

Grace rose and placed her hand in the crook. Her eyes widened when he pulled his arm closer to his body. Without thought, her hand tightened. When she looked up, his brown eyes darkened as he smiled. They sauntered down the long room, making pleasantries about the day's weather. The length of the space allowed for quiet discussion without being overheard. After a turnabout, Grace took a deep breath and blurted out what had been on her mind.

"It was kind of you to allow Eliza to use your given name. Under the circumstances, I can understand how the use of your title might be disconcerting."

"A small enough gesture. She was devastated, you know. That may have been one reason I offered. Her grief was sincere, and I imagine looking into the twin of your dead husband would be alarming enough. My father was not pleased but then he rarely is." He looked down, considering her. "Do you disapprove?"

"While I believe in protocol for many things, this situation is not one of them. It was a thoughtful token that eased her pain," she explained. "I cannot disapprove of that."

"Are you enjoying your visit so far?" They passed the others as they looped around the room. Eliza grinned at her, her eyebrows raised.

"Indeed, sir. Falsbury is stately, yet provokes the imagination." Grace loved this old castle. The unexpected hiding places in dark passages, ancient stones, and narrow winding stairs.

"Let me guess, the turrets and arrow slits have you fancying kings and queens with their banners, knights in battle, all the medieval romantic notions," he said.

"I hate to sound a bore, but I can't imagine war being romantic." He did not respond at first. She peeked at him under her lashes and he halted. His gaze locked with hers, the pain evident in his eyes. "No, I can see it was not."

"I don't think I could ever describe the true horror of battle. The sounds, the smells, the wrenching of one's soul when another life is taken." His face paled. "The aftermath may be even worse than the actual killing."

The agony on his face shocked her. He stood there, looking at her but not seeing her. His mind was in a terrible place, caught in a poignant memory.

Grace wanted to hold him, comfort him, murmur soft words that the terror would fade. But she could not play him false. He deserved better than that, so she only stood quietly with a slight smile and waited for him to come back. His head jerked, his eyes focusing on her face. With a slight pressure on his arm, she stepped forward and they resumed their pace.

"You make a fine figure on a horse. I would like to see you on a white steed, my lord," she remarked, hoping to pull him from his wretched thoughts.

"And you, my lady, make a fine figure at any time and any place." He bowed, his previous humor returning. "I see you were reading Byron. A fan like most of the young ladies, I presume?"

With a giggle, she shook her head. "I do enjoy his prose. However, I do not carry his portrait in a locket so I may look at him and swoon. And yes, I have seen it happen."

"I am cheered you are not jingle-brained, Lady Grace. In the military there are two kind of women, and neither are fatwits." He seemed to consider her. "I believe you would fare well as a soldier's wife."

"I believe that is a compliment. Why do you think so?"

"It is a different strain of female that will follow her husband to war. Not that they don't bring along fineries, or make friends in nearby cities and attend events, for that is all a needed distraction from the real issue."

She waited until they had once again passed her father and the ladies. "Which is?"

"The reason such women come along is to know what happened. They want the last word, the last look, the last kiss they can steal from fate before their husbands raise sword and pistol and charge against the enemy. I've seen wives follow their men into the fray." He gave her a mischievous smirk. "I believe you might have been that sort of woman."

"Oh my. Pistol waving above my head, screaming to stand down or face my fury." Grace rolled her eyes. "I'm sure I would have been a terror."

"Perhaps not, but you have the strength and courage for the job."

His words filled her with pride. She enjoyed this man, and worried for him. Papa had always said a man never knows the effects of war until he has come home. She wondered what ghosts chased Lord Sunderland.

Grace and the earl continued their evening strolls, in either the drawing room or the garden on cooler nights, discussing current events and politics, literature and music. Perhaps there was no harm in some mild flirtation with the earl. Eliza praised him as considerate and understanding. "And as handsome as Lord Byron if not as poetic."

Papa had noticed their mutual appreciation. If he thought there was a possibility of a match between them, would he not drop the subject of suitors, at least until Eliza gave birth? If Eliza had a son and heir, Sunderland would probably return to his old life and she would return to hers. They could both go their own ways, no harm done.

But if she had a girl? The earl would be forced to marry just as his brother had. Did he consider her a prospect? If she did have to marry someone, he would indeed be a good candidate. Her body heated at the thought of his intimate touch, his fingers stroking her skin, his lips trailing hot kisses along her neck and finally claiming...

"Grace! Have you heard a word I've said?" Eliza asked sharply. "You're wearing the most ridiculous expression."

She jumped, guilty at the scandalous thoughts running through her mind. "My mind was elsewhere."

"On Kit, I would wager. Don't think I haven't noticed the way his eyes light up when you enter a room, or the pink in your cheeks when he teases you." Eliza linked arms and pulled her from the library. "With all your common sense, you were blushing this morning at breakfast when he said your morning dress brought out the gold flecks in your green eyes."

"It was only flummery," she mumbled.

"I didn't warrant any compliments," Eliza argued. "Oh cousin, do you think a match is possible? He is such a good fellow. How many men would be so kind to a woman who might steal their title from them in a few short months? Never a harsh word, always asking about the baby and my health."

"I'm happy you've found a better life." Grace gave her a squeeze as they ambled down the hall. "And I admit I enjoy the attention. For the first time in my life, I understand why girls swoon and whisper about this man or that. But I still have no desire to marry."

"Gracie, how can you say that when your parents were so devoted to each other?"

"Where did it get my mother? Do you remember what my father went through when she died?" She shook her head, her lips pressed together. "And I could never leave Sammy. Papa would be devastated without me to run the house. He's just worried about my future."

"Or his. He might marry again."

Eliza couldn't have hurt her more with a knife to the heart. "What? Do you think he wants another wife?"

Her cousin stopped and placed a hand on Grace's cheek. "He's still a handsome man and in good health. Why should he be alone when he has so much more to give?"

Grace was horrified. It had never occurred to her that her father might consider remarrying. Is that why he was so adamant to find a match? Her world tilted as she mulled the possibility. How selfish she had been. Everyone's life did not revolve around her, but her world revolved around them. She had made sure of that, so another kind of existence would never tempt her. And love would never rule her heart. "Sammy would have a real mother, not a sister usurping the role." Tears pricked her eyes. "I'm afraid my ego has blinded me when it comes to my family."

"No, no. They love you, Gracie. Where would they have been without you the past five years? But we grow and change and move on, don't we? That's no one's fault, it's just life."

"I suppose." How could she tell Eliza that she also feared childbirth? It might frighten her cousin and harm the baby. "Let's enjoy our visit together for now and worry about the rest later. Agreed?"

"Agreed. Now, let's find Sammy and give your father a reprieve until dinner."

They found Sammy and Papa out on the lawn, playing Battledore and Shuttlecock. Eliza clapped as they batted the shuttlecock back and forth between the paddles. "Twenty-one, twenty-two, twenty-three," she cried. "The last time I tried this, my partner and I couldn't keep it up more than three or four passes."

Lord Boldon stretched toward the ground to save the weighted feathers, his strike somewhat haphazard but successful. Sammy jumped as high as he could and missed. "Ha! You spoke too soon, Eliza my dear." He waved his paddle. "Another go, son?"

Grace watched the two of them as they played. Her father had hung his coat on a branch of a nearby Rowan tree, his light brown hair darkened by sweat. He moved like a younger man, his face alight with pleasure as he swung the battledore up. Her mind wandered back to the earlier conversation. The Earl of Boldon was a passionate, vibrant aristocrat with lands and wealth. Why hadn't it occurred to her he might love again? The knot in her stomach stretched and tightened. Marriage was not an unreasonable expectation for any daughter. She enjoyed dancing and light flirtation, not that she'd had much experience with the latter. The social events within ames-ace of Boldon were somewhat limited but country dances were popular. Many were held on their own estate.

Her life would be so different, wouldn't it? She had grown used to her independence. Papa never questioned her expenditures; in fact, she kept the household books. A husband would expect her to be obedient and mind her words. She could never act like one of those dimwitted debutantes, always in agreement with the man, their eyes cast downward. Nor could she be one of the brazen girls who openly trifled with men and quickly earned a reputation.

Sammy fulfilled her maternal longings. She couldn't imagine not seeing her brother every day.

Even if her father didn't need her, Sammy would be heartbroken. And would a second wife want to raise another woman's child? *Stop it!* She scolded herself. *Who could not become attached to that little boy? Take off the blinders and stop making excuses.*

"Do you play, Lady Grace?"

She closed her eyes, his breath warm against her temple. The winged creatures took flight in her belly again. How did he manage to keep slipping up beside her without notice? "Yes, I'm rather good. And you?"

"I haven't played since I was a boy."

She saw him standing in her side vision, his hands clasped behind his back. Black suited him, made him more enigmatic. "Perhaps we would be evenly matched then?"

"Ha! I'd pull caps with you on that. I doubt I would make a good show of it." He tilted his head and studied her. "Do you enjoy physical exercise...other than walking? Do you ride?"

"Of course, but my mare was a bit long in the tooth to bring. Papa mentioned something about finding me a nice mount soon. He said Lord Falsbury would be arriving soon?"

"Unfortunately, I just got a letter from him this morning. He won't be here for another week or two. The estate in the south of London needs more repairs than he thought. Finding good tradesmen these days you can trust isn't easy." He watched the game for a moment. "I'd be happy to take you and Lord Boldon on a tour of our lands."

Those ridiculous wings began again in her stomach, along with the silly smile. She looked over at Eliza, an *I-told-you-so* smirk on her face. "That would be very generous of you, my lord. I'm sure the views are beautiful."

He grinned, his eyes crinkling in jest as his gaze swept from her head to her shoes and back up. "Yes, the view is quite lovely."

"And suddenly you just know...it's time to start something new and trust the magic of beginnings."

Meister Eckhart

Chapter Eleven

Mid July 1815

Kit had chosen a little red roan mare for the ride. When the groom retrieved the sidesaddle, Lord Boldon laughed. "If it wouldn't appall you, put an astride saddle on her. I'm an overly indulgent father, I admit. If we are not riding in a group, and on our own property, I allow it."

He nodded to the groom. "May I ask if I will next see your daughter in a pair of buckskins and Hessians?" The idea wasn't appalling at all. The sight of Lady Grace's backside, molded by a pair of men's breeches made his blood hot.

Boldon laughed. "No, no. I think if you are considering furthering your...friendship with my daughter, there are certain aspects of her personality you should be aware of sooner than later." With that tidbit, he turned and mounted his bay gelding, putting him through several paces.

Lady Grace approached in a forest green riding habit and matching hat with a feather that swished back and forth as she moved. The long skirt billowed around her, but the bodice was snug. She smiled and waved as she approached.

Kit rubbed the horse's nose as the groom saddled her. "Oh, how I'd love to be you today. Take good care of the lady," he whispered in the animal's ear, "or you answer to me."

"I hope I didn't make you wait." She circled the mare, a deliberate eye to the mare's legs and haunches. "She looks sturdy, and lovely coloring."

"Your father said you would like her." She intrigued him with her combination of intelligence, beauty, and maternal tendencies. And athletic? He wanted to see her gallop across a field and jump a hedge. *And if the hat blows off, so much the better*.

Lady Grace clapped her hands when she noticed the saddle then bit her lip. "So you've discovered my secret."

"Blackmail... I may need a second career if Eliza has a boy." He beckoned to the groom, who appeared a moment later with his black stallion.

Lady Grace's eyes lit up at the sight of the horse. "There are some prime bits of blood in your stable, my lord. Your stallion is no exception. What is his name?"

"Lance," he answered. "When I bought him at Tattersall's, the man's daughter had named him Lancelot. My regiment would have laughed me off the battlefield. So I kept Lance and chopped the lot."

Her eyes lit with humor. "Now *I* have information not commonly known. And the mare?"

"This is Dottie, so called because of the speckled coat." He motioned to the horse. "Would you like help up or do you prefer a mounting block?"

"Your assistance, my lord, would be much appreciated." She tossed her crop into her right hand. Kit cupped his hands and Grace placed her foot within it. He gave her gentle boost up, and she swung into the saddle with ease.

The day was cloudy and threatened rain as the three of them and the estate manager set off. They traveled at a steady trot for the first quarter of an hour. Satisfied that Grace was as competent as predicted, he issued a challenge. "Let's race to the hedges." He pointed in the direction of a field of grazing sheep, goading her with a look.

"I'm out," called Lord Boldon then looked toward the estate manager. "Let's take a look at the sheep while they play. I'm thinking of adding a herd myself."

"Happy to, my lord," the man answered and the two trotted off.

"The hedge is the finish line? And the winner?" Grace challenged him back.

"Yes, and the loser forfeits dessert at dinner."

"Never! On the count of three. One, two—"

She smacked her mare with the crop and with a leap, the animal bolted. Laughter floated behind her. He made an indignant sound and chased after her. The two animals ran neck and neck for a few moments. The sound of hoofbeats pounding the earth filled his ears, scraps of dirt and clover left in their wake. Lady Grace was an excellent rider, gripping the horse with her legs, bent forward slightly with a light hand on the reins, giving the mare her head. Exhilaration colored her face. She was stunning. Then Kit focused on the race, and his larger steed took the lead. He pulled up in front of the hedges, turned his horse on its hindquarters, and waited for the loser with a grin.

A blur of horse and rider whirred past his head, taking the hedge in a graceful arc. She pulled back on the reins, squeezed with her right leg, and the horse pivoted on its hindquarters. With a kick of both boots and light smack of the crop, they reversed direction. Kit stood his ground as Lady Grace leapt over the hedge again, her skirts flying behind her, cheeks bright with excitement. They slid to a stop, the mare's nostrils flaring, and turned to face him.

"If you are trying to impress me because you lost the race, you have succeeded. Nicely done, my lady." He bowed from the saddle. "However, you lost."

"Did you not say the hedge was the finish line?" One eyebrow arched arrogantly.

"Yes, but—"

"I crossed the finish line. You did not. It is you who shall forfeit his very favorite sweetmeat to me." The smugness in her eyes was irritating and delicious. He wanted to kiss that look off her face.

His laugh was loud and spontaneous. He'd been duped. "I concede to a clever opponent."

They fell in next to each other at a brisk walk and turned toward the herd of sheep. "My brother's admiration for you grows each day," she commented as they slowly made their way across the pasture. "I wouldn't have taken you for a man who enjoys children."

"I haven't had much experience with them, to tell the truth. He's brought back some of my best memories playing here as a child with Carson. Believe me, he's given far more to me these past weeks than I have given him." Sammy had driven back the darkness of grief and brought the light of remembrance to the forefront. Now he remembered the laughter, the mischief, the bond he and Carson had shared. The troubled, self-destructive brother was fading to the background. Kit was thankful to the boy for that.

"What was it like growing up as a twin?"

People were always curious about twins and assumed that if two people looked alike, they were alike. "Wonderful and ghastly," he answered with a grin. "Our father took little notice of us during our childhood. Our mother believed a governess had more experience at raising children. But we were never lonely because we had each other. We were confidantes and the best of friends. Carson was corky as a child, moving from one activity to another, never finishing one project before starting another, pulling terrible pranks on family and guests. I was often blamed for his tricks, or put myself in the middle to save his hide."

"So he became the buck and you the Corinthian."

"Ha! Yes, my brother never slowed in his pursuit of pleasure. His reputation for debauchery began at university, never refusing a challenge or wager. He was a better horseman than me, but I excelled at archery and shooting." It had been a sore spot of Carson's that his aim was inferior to Kit's. "He had his faults but he was a gentle soul at heart and his loyalty unwavering once given."

"You were close but very different, it appears." She saw past his mask, exposing his secrets, enticing him to trust her.

"I wish others had noticed the disparity. I struggled against Carson's reputation until I took my commission. His notoriety was connected to one face, and I happened to have the same appearance." He grimaced, remembering the frustration of the whispers and looks when he was mistaken for his brother.

"Did you envy him the title?"

"Never. He hated the responsibility of being the heir and tried several times over the years to switch places. It would never have worked, of course, though he was right. He was better suited to the role of second son." The old regret niggled at his conscience.

"Your grief is still raw." The sympathy in her voice made him blink. "The loss must have been devastating."

"I cannot explain it. The bond we possessed went beyond familial love. We knew each other's thoughts, could give a warning or comfort with a look. He was my other half, and I don't know if I will ever be whole again." He gripped the reins as he spoke, the words forming without his consent. Lady Grace did not want to hear the melancholy whining of her host. "I apologize, my lady, I'm not usually a mawkish rattle with my guests."

She laid a hand on his rein, her green eyes misty as she slowed the horse to a sedate walk. "My lord, there is nothing insipid about your loss. I understand the hollowness that comes with losing one so close to your heart. My mother was my closest friend. I was only fifteen when she died and will never fill the void from her death."

Her empathy eased the ache. The caress of her soft tone, the offer of comfort in her eyes made him long to reach out and pull her from her horse. Kit wanted to bury his face in her hair, breathe in her scent of vanilla and citrus, press her warm body against his.

"Thank you." He took a deep breath, his heart lighter when she withdrew her hand. "It seems we have much in common, my lady. How did you cope?"

She gazed at her father as they grew closer. "My father was inconsolable for weeks. Between him and an infant, I stayed busy. My mother had prepared me. I knew how to run a household, but the task was daunting without her help or advice. But I managed."

"Your father placed a great deal of responsibility on your shoulders." He admired her audacity. Many girls that age would have wallowed in self-pity. "It shaped your character and made you independent."

"Too much, I fear." Her grin was contagious, and he smiled back.

"How so?"

"It has made me cautious of marriage. I do not want to be under the thumb of some husband who wishes me to obey his every wish. Most men expect a woman to be bacon-brained and be content with bearing his children and creating lovely needlework." She reached out to stroke the mare's neck. "I cannot see myself in such a role. I'd rather lose my head than my independence."

"So you've found ways to avoid a season in London in order to preserve your pretty head." She was a complex, captivating female who presented a challenge to any man preferring a wife with substance. He desired her; he liked her. It was an unsettling combination.

A raindrop plopped on her skirt, making a black circle against the green material. "It appears the weather may cool our horses for us, my lord." They both squinted at the dark, swollen clouds hanging low in the sky. Grace hadn't noticed them before. The moisture cooled her heated skin. Lord Sunderland's confession had touched her. There was so much more to this man than what he chose to reveal. The earl was a complicated man. She envied his strength and steadfastness. He'd spoken of his brother's loyalty, but he embodied that trait.

His handsome face, etched with remorse and sorrow, had brought tears to her eyes. How she had wanted to wrap her arms around him, stroke his dark hair, and murmur soothing words in his ear. A man with such pride, who could open his soul as Sunderland had, sent a wave of compassion and longing through her body. And now he was reading her like a well-practiced poem.

"I am afraid if I did accept a proposal, I'd end up the jilt and ruin my family's reputation. So I will sacrifice my matrimonial happiness for the name of future generations." She pressed her lips together, determined not to giggle at her own folly.

"You are educated in the subject of rationalization, I see," he teased.

"So I've been told before," she agreed. "I would lose more than I gain by marriage. Not only my independence is at stake, but my family. There is no one to run the household, be a mother to Sammy, or a companion to my father."

"Not even a duke could persuade you?" he asked, his voice low and husky.

"It depends."

"On his appearance, his wealth, or both?" His tone had changed to irritation and she bit back the grin.

"On his willingness to live at Boldon. I would refuse to be a tenant for life anywhere else."

Grace realized her father and the estate manager had been joined by two more riders. An older woman, still lovely with pale hair and blue eyes, sat sidesaddle on a smart chestnut with another man on a large gray horse.

"Did you enjoy your gallop?" her father asked as they joined the foursome. "May I introduce Lady Rafferton? We met in London last year, and she lives on the neighboring estate." She was a lady of quality, judging by the navy riding habit and hat. Her fine leather gloves held the reins with the ease of one used to being on a horse. The light-haired man next to her, dressed in a plain shirt and coat, must be a manager or groom.

Lord Sunderland tipped his hat. "Lady Rafferton, it has been too many years. You are lovely as ever."

"How kind. I believe you grow more handsome each time I see you," she quipped back, bestowing him with a gracious smile. "I am planning to visit your mother next week to offer my condolences. I have only just returned from Scotland, where my daughter was married. I hope we will have a chance to talk longer. It appears the weather is interrupting this time."

A knot wrapped around Grace's stomach and squeezed. He was flirting with this beautiful creature, moments after his compliments to her. The rake. What flummery. *Oh god. Why do you care?* she thought. They made their farewells and headed back to Falsbury. Jealousy burned her throat, a new sensation. She didn't like it.

Determined to rid herself of the disagreeable emotion, she confronted the earl. "It seems the lady is an admirer, my lord." She clenched her jaw at his chuckle, and clucked to her horse to pass him by. His teasing would not work this time.

"Lady Rafferton is a close friend of my mother. She appears younger but is ten years my senior." He pulled up next to her, ignoring her cut. "It is humiliating to remember how smitten I was as a boy."

Unexplained relief bubbled up inside her, and she rewarded his words with a brilliant smile. His olive skin, still dark from his military years on the field, made the cream-colored cravat almost white. Her eyes lingered on the wide mouth and firm lips that now softened in a smile, revealing his pearly teeth. God help her. She'd have to proceed with care, or this *harmless* flirtation might snare her heart. That was not something she cared to risk.

"The great art of life is sensation, to feel that we exist, even in pain."

Lord Byron

Chapter Twelve

Late July 1815

Kit strolled into the drawing room, scanning the small group for Lady Grace. She was never far from his mind, intruding on his thoughts throughout the day. Her satin skin and yielding lips. That body wrapped in a snug riding habit, her chest heaving after a long canter and those liquid green eyes laughing at him, sent his blood rushing. Last night she invaded his dreams, though he admitted it was a sight better than the nightmares he was accustomed to after battle.

They had been out for a ride when it began to rain. A cabin had been close by, and Kit had started a fire. When he turned, she had peeled the wet clothes from her body. A goddess with her arms held out to him, the fire casting golden shadows against her skin. He had woken this morning drenched and panting. Thinking of the dream now, a powerful lust surged through his loins. *Cold ice cream from*

Gunter's, he thought. No, not chilling enough. *A dip in the lake in April. Ah, that's better.*

Once in control of his desire, he paused beside the rosewood sofa table to pour a glass of burgundy. Only his mother and another female perched on the sofa. She beckoned to her son with excitement. "Do you remember Lady Rafferton? She stopped to offer her condolences."

"Yes, we met up last week when I was out for a ride with Lord Boldon and Lady Grace." The viscountess lived on a neighboring estate and was a frequent visitor. They often joined one another's hunts in the fall. He was impressed again by her youthful appearance. Blonde waves swept above a slender neck, curls strategically loosened around the face and nape. A gown of pale rose, with the same flower embroidered across the hem, hugged a still slender figure. He took her extended hand, bowed low, and placed a kiss on her gloved fingers. "I could never forget the woman who broke my heart as a boy by marrying Lord Rafferton."

"And now you have grown into a man yourself. I wager you have most of the London debutantes smelling of April and May." Her smile faded, her blue eyes sincere. "I do apologize for not coming sooner. Horrible business for your family."

He inclined his head. "And your husband? He is well?"

"Oh dear, you didn't know? He's been gone...two years?" Lady Falsbury looked at her friend, eyebrows raised.

"Three. I am a widow now, my lord. So you see? Your broken heart may at last mend." She tapped her fan against his forearm. "Are you here for long or just a brief visit?"

"Well, I..."

A rustling came from the corner near a Greek bust of Helen. The heavy velvet drapes rustled then a sneeze echoed across the room.

Kit put a finger to his lips, handed his glass off to his mother, and motioned for them to keep talking. "It depends on if my father needs me to help with that estate south of London." He moved to the corner.

"I doubt if he makes it here at all. He'll end up meeting us in Brighton. That man cannot allow anyone to assume his business. Has to have a finger in every pot."

Kit peered behind an ottoman. Two golden brown orbs blinked back at him. "What have we here? A fugitive highwayman?" He kicked away the cushioned seat. "Ladies, remove yourselves. My sword, load my pistol!"

A squeak sounded from the shadows, and then Sammy rose, his bottom lip stuck out, eyes downcast. "It's only me."

"Good gracious, boy. What are you doing hiding in here?" asked Lady Falsbury.

"Papa wanted me to bathe before he dressed for dinner. If he can't find me, I won't have to." He kicked at the ottoman. "I hate baths."

"You don't look so dirty to me," coaxed Lady Rafferton. "Come here and let me smell you."

The boy looked up, hope brightening his face. He ran to the woman, stuck his head under her nose, and then presented his armpits. With a straight face, she sniffed his hair and then wrinkled her nose as he raised his arms. "I'd say the hair isn't bad but the rest is a bit ripe." She laughed at his forlorn look. "However, I've smelled much worse."

The child nodded his head up and down. "That's what I said." He sat down next to her. "I haven't seen you before."

"This is our neighbor and one of my closest confidantes," Lady Falsbury answered. "And this is Samuel, Lady Eliza's cousin."

"Pleased to make your acquaintance, my lord," she responded with a nod. "I've heard much about you."

The boy stood and gave her a deep bow. "At your service, madam."

"Why thank you, kind sir," she replied, inclining her head as Sammy turned back to Kit.

"She broke your heart? Will she fix it? You have to help me with my theater tomorrow. The play has the"—he put his hands on each side of his mouth and whispered loudly—"explosion at the end." His eyes moved sideways to see if the women had heard. "It's a surprise I'm planning for everyone."

"I love surprises," said Lady Rafferton.

"You must come. We've been practicing *The Miller and His Men*. Everyone will be there."

"Samuel," bellowed a voice from the door. "I have had quite enough of your impudence. Come to your room *now*!"

Sammy cringed. "Please say you'll come?"

Lord Boldon came up behind the boy. "Beg your pardon, my ladies, but I must remove my son in all haste," he muttered through clenched teeth as bowed to the women. "It is good to see you again, Lady Rafferton."

Lady Grace and Lady Eliza entered close behind, also searching for the filthy youngster. As Boldon dragged his unwilling son from the room, the boy choked out, "You will come, won't you my lady? We have colored sheets for the background. And Eliza will accompany us on the pianoforte." His tawny head disappeared around the corner.

"He stretches one's patience, but he is sweet-natured child," Lady Grace apologized for her younger brother.

"I think he's refreshing," said Lady Rafferton. "He reminds me of my youngest son. He's still a constant worry, either finding trouble in London and the gaming-hells or making the ladies swoon at the seaside resorts."

"How many children do you have, my lady?"

"A daughter, who is a gift from heaven though recently married and gone from me, and three sons. The eldest is my stepson and has assumed the title, the second is a lieutenant colonel, and my youngest..." She shook her head. "He just finished university and applied to one of the Inns of Court."

"He wants to be a barrister?" Lady Eliza asked. "I think the study of law and the courts is fascinating. You don't approve?"

"If he's in earnest, yes. If it's an excuse to squander his allowance on Cyprians in the foyer of Covent Garden, no. But as my youngest, he knows how to get around me." She gathered her reticule and bestowed a kiss on each of her friend's cheeks. "Now, I must be off. It was lovely to meet all of you."

"You must stay for dinner," Lady Falsbury demanded.

"I wish I could. However, I do believe I'll take Samuel up on his invitation tomorrow."

Kit chuckled as he and Lady Grace groaned at the same time. "I cannot guarantee the performance. Except for the explosion, the author would barely recognize his work. The young man has condensed most of it to get to the good part, as he puts it."

"Don't be fooled, my lady. Lord Sunderland is an excellent and brave hero." The smile Grace bestowed upon him was warm and playful. He looked to the ceiling and once again thought of a freezing swim in April.

Grace closed her eyes and said a quick prayer that all went well. It had taken them a week of coloring and cutting and pasting to prepare for the play. Lord Sunderland's infinite patience had surprised her. He seemed to know just when Sammy had had enough, and they would go outside and romp on the lawn to expel the boy's energy. The juvenile drama put her in the earl's constant vicinity each afternoon. That fact was the only reason she might be disappointed after the performance.

She had learned his mannerisms: he stroked his chin in deep thought, his jaw ticked when he was irritated, humor made his eyes sparkle, and flirting made them darken. When truly amused, a deep rumble would start low in his chest and come out a husky, masculine laugh that made her skin tingle. Sometimes he teased her, and his look seemed so intimate, she thought he would reach out and take her hand.

"Gracie, hurry. We don't have long."

Lady Falsbury had put her foot down and refused to allow the gunpowder in the drawing room. A tent had been set up outside the drawing room window, so Eliza would be able to provide the music from inside. The attendants would be under shade, and if anything went wrong, the tiny theater and perhaps the lawn would be the only casualties.

At least twenty chairs had been set up. Eliza had requested some of the staff to come and watch so there would be enough for an audience. Samuel surveyed the scene and nodded in approval. He placed the sturdy paper characters on their stands and pushed them along the slits in the board until they were center stage. The villain Grindoff stood with his gang of thieves, plotting against the count. Sammy pushed the background along another slit, depicting the thieves' secret hideout. Then he placed the sheets for the corresponding scenes behind that.

"Are we too early?" asked their father, standing with Lady Falsbury on his arm. "Shall we find our own seats or is there an escort?"

"I hadn't thought of that." Sammy rubbed his jaw in a perfect imitation of Lord Sunderland.

Grace hid her smile. "There are three places of honor in the front, Papa," she informed him.

As they both settled themselves, the servants arrived one by one and filled the back rows. Sammy went to the open window and called up, "Start the waiting music, Eliza."

"Yes, my lord," came a muffled reply.

"She's here, she's here," cried Sammy. "Lady Rafferton is coming."

The marchioness patted Lord Boldon's arm. "Would you escort my dear friend?"

"Of course, I'd be happy to."

Grace watched her father walk away, his confident, long stride carrying him quickly to the long drive. When he reemerged with the viscountess on his arm, they were both laughing. Before she could even consider the pair, a shadow fell over her. His nearness was alluring and disturbing at the same time. Earthy mint and faint orange tickled her nose and sent her pulse into a staccato rhythm. The scent would forever bring to mind Lord Sunderland and this most excellent summer.

"Claudine, my love. I have come to make you mine." He bowed, a smirk on his lips as he recited a line from the play. "But first, mademoiselle, I must play with fire."

"Please, my dear Lothair, do be careful. I shall die of a broken heart if you do not return." She placed her hand on her forehead and attempted a heroine's dramatic pose.

He leaned close and whispered, "Tell me true, my darling."

She saw the change in his eyes, the heat that deepened the brown to clear midnight sky. A shiver passed over her. Grace realized how much she would miss this man when she went home next week. He had attached himself to her daily routine, and the thought he would no longer be a part of her day, left a place in her heart empty.

The earl gave her a half smile then took her arm. "We'd better get in place behind the theater."

The audience quieted and Sammy stood before them. Eliza's introduction sonata floated through the window. "Our play begins with the evil Grindoff. He worked for the count until he was discovered to be untrustworthy. Sent away in disgrace, he disguised himself as a miller."

Kit moved the miller back and forth.

"Grindoff had a plan. First, he gathered a gang of thieves."

Grace wiggled the group of paper men.

"He would trick the richest villager, take his money and his beautiful daughter, Claudine."

Grace picked up the paper girl and slid her into the theater. "No good sir," she said to the villain, "I have already given my heart to Lothair."

Lothair appeared alongside Claudine. Another female character slid in next to Grindoff. "You oaf, I am your woman. How can you betray me?" Grace did her best to sound like a vixen.

Sunderland was so close, she could feel the heat emanating from his body. Or was that hers? He made her senses come alive. As the play continued, she was acutely aware of the brush of his sleeve, the skim of his finger against her hand. The blades of grass beneath her each made their own cool dent against her stockings. The breeze rustled loose curls against her neck, tickling and teasing her skin. His nearness sent ripples of sensation through her body. It was a new feeling, this desire, this physical need for someone.

It became difficult to remember her lines; her breathing grew more rapid. Once she lost her balance, but he caught her. His hands grasped her waist and lingered, the pressure intimate and inviting. The single touch burned through the layers of her muslin dress, petticoats, and chemise. Startled, she watched his mouth curl, transfixed as it slanted up, white teeth flashing between firm, sensual lips. In her mind, his head tipped for a kiss... Sunderland's elbow unromantically poked her side when she missed her cue, and the poor paper count crumpled in her fist.

"I shall find them out, sweet Claudine. Wait for me."

He gave her a curious look as she searched her brain for the next line. "Take care, Grindoff's gang is a dangerous bunch."

The rest of the play went off perfectly. Grace focused on her lines and did not allow her thoughts to stray again. Lothair was discovered in the thieves' cave but rescued by the spurned lady of Grindoff. As the gang realized they had been found out, they rushed after Lothair.

"He ran across the bridge with great speed—"

Sunderland tried to move the figure up along the bridge, lost his grip, and Lothair clattered to the stage floor. Sammy never lost a beat. "...and tripped and fell over the side. But he was a strong swimmer and pulled himself to shore."

The earl bobbed Lothair to the other side of the bridge and called, "Fire the bridge! Fire the bridge!"

Grace pushed the gang of thieves toward the bridge. Sammy ran behind the theater to join them, pulsating with excitement. A small pile of gunpowder lay inside a tin cup, a string hanging across the edge. Sunderland dipped a match head into a small asbestos bottle of sulfuric acid to produce a flame. He handed it to a solemn Sammy, who set the small flame to the wick. It sizzled and sparked red as it moved inside the cup. *Boom!* Red and yellow flashed through the smoky explosion. Embers burned the edges of the theater and the earl squashed the would-be fire out using his hands and several of the other characters. The three actors coughed and spluttered. Grace used one of the backdrops to fan away the smoke.

The audience gasped and clapped while Sammy jumped with delight, his arms flailing above his head. Then remembering his role, he stood before the group again. "Grindoff is seized and the thieves run away to whence they came." He looked over his shoulder at Sunderland and his sister. "Lothair returned to Claudine. They embraced." He waited for the two singed characters to touch. "And lived happily ever after. The end."

Sammy motioned his actors to join him. They all clasped hands and took a bow together.

"Brava! Bravo!"

"Magnificent!"

The boy beamed as everyone stood for a standing ovation. Grace stood with one hand clasped in Sammy's and the other in the earl's. She felt moistness in his palm and opened his palm for inspection. She wondered what the roughness of those fingertips would feel like against her cheek, her neck until she saw the oozing burn. "You have blisters," she gasped.

"It's nothing. I'm fine."

"If not treated, it could become inflamed. Please, come to the kitchen, and I'll apply a salve."

"I was hoping you'd say that."

"He then, with great presence of mind, put a stop to any further recriminations by kissing her; and his indignant betrothed, apparently feeling that he was too deeply sunk in depravity to be reclaimable, abandoned (for the time being, at all events) any further attempt to bring him to a sense of his iniquity."

Georgette Heyer, *Sylvester*

Chapter Thirteen

Mrs. Whitten once again came to their rescue. Following them after the production, the cook sent a boy to the icehouse for a cup of shavings off the huge block stored underground. Kit found himself once again at the stain-darkened table. He held the chips in a cloth against his palm, while Grace oversaw the tobacco poultice made with yesterday's moistened bread, meal, and the plant leaves. He studied the silver serving platters and porcelain dishes along the wall shelves, the pots hanging from the ceiling, and the ceramic jar near the copper-lined sink. The hiding place for Mrs. Whitten's dry sweetmeats. His mouth watered. When his hand was numb, she took a needle and pierced the blisters then applied the poultice. He winced once when she missed the blister and the point went deeper into his hand. The look of pain on her face was much worse than what he had suffered. He had been foolish to make notice of it and cause her concern.

"Have I thanked you properly for all your attention to Sammy? You are a hero to him, equal only to my father in his eyes." Grace kept her eyes on the blisters, the needle steady in her small capable hand. Her head was bent low as she concentrated. She was so close he had to move but a few inches and his mouth would be on her cheek. If she turned her head, it would be her lips.

"That depends on what you consider a proper thank you." He goaded her, he knew. But time was no longer on his side. She returned to her own estates in a few short days, and he would be left...alone. He needed to tell her how he felt, that he couldn't imagine not seeing her again, that he had grown fond of her. More than fond.

Grinning, she said drolly, "Perhaps Mrs. Whitten could witness a proper thank you, if you described such a thing to her."

Embarrassment crept up his neck as the image of her gratitude formed in his mind. No, he certainly didn't want any witnesses. She smirked at his silence, a raised eyebrow telling him that she had seen through his ploy.

"When this begins to hurt again, add more ice and then another poultice. Mrs. Whitten has agreed to make up more for you."

He looked over Grace's shoulder and saw the cook was busy at the other end of the room. "Lady Eliza and Sammy will be here soon. I need to speak with you privately."

A startled look passed over her face, and she repeated his motion, glancing over her shoulder to see who was close. "Yes, my lord?"

"I fear a fit of the blue devils when you leave Falsbury at the end of the week." He'd said it. Told her he had grown attached. In a roundabout sort of way.

Mrs. Whitten interrupted them. "I need to fetch some more lard to finish these poultices, my lady. I'll be right back." They were alone.

"I-I have grown used to your company also." In those deep emerald eyes, he saw it: love, fear, hesitation. The world stood still as the breath was sucked out of him; nothing existed but the two of them. With a strange certainty, he knew they shared the first emotion. It hit him as hard and fast as an enemy ambush. He'd never experienced this kind of romantic love. The only people in the world that he'd associated the word with were his mother and Carson. Yes, and now Grace. This helped him understand the second emotion. It was frightening indeed. The void that Carson had left in his soul only resulted from true affection. And they both recognized they had come too far to pretend otherwise.

"Lady Grace, I ask your permission to speak with your father. I would like—no, I *need* to see you again. Might you possibly feel the same?" He was a Johnny Raw once more, kissing his first girl.

Her scrutiny made him shift in his seat, and the needle poked through his skin again. He made a small noise, and their attention was drawn to the drop of blood that spread in his palm. A tear fell and mixed with the deep red, forming a tiny pink puddle between the two blisters. His chest tightened, not understanding the meaning of it.

Grace swiped at her eyes with the back of a hand. Her voice was steady when she spoke but her gaze remained lowered. "I am honored by your request. In truth, if it were not for my situation, I would welcome your courtship. But in my present position, I cannot."

"If it's concern over my attitude as a husband, I may not be as doting as your father but I certainly won't quash your spirit."

"It is too much to risk." Her head snapped up, and the words came out in a rush, passionate and urgent. "It is not only my independence. There is my father, he leans on me for companionship, to run the household, help him plan events and act as hostess. Who would take care of Sammy? I am like a mother to him. The thought of leaving..."

"Do you hold me in your affections, Lady Grace?" This was the issue. The rest could be addressed, but if she did not have the same feelings that he did then it was all pointless. Her gaze drifted again to his palm, pretending to fiddle with the burn.

"Mrs. Whitten should be back any moment and I'll apply the poultice."

His mouth fell open. She would ignore him. She would not answer him. She would pretend as if this discussion had not happened. "By god, I won't allow it."

He stood, the chair clattering against the stone floor. She gasped. Her glistening green eyes blinked at the sudden movement. One arm came around her waist and yanked her against him; the trembling lips undid him. His last shred of self-restraint drained from his body. Kit dipped his head and claimed her mouth, soft and yielding. Her curves fit against him as if they had been cut from one mold. He eased up slightly and brushed his lips against hers, caressing and coaxing. A tremor passed through him as she sighed, her breath mingling with his. Citrus and vanilla enveloped him, intoxicated him. She was everything he had dreamed of. She was nothing he had expected.

He lifted his head, scrambling for a pittance of sanity but her arms went around his neck. The slight surrender sent a tremor down his length, his trousers tightening with desire. Kit buried his head in her neck, trailing hot kisses up the pale skin, feeling her pulse beneath his lips. He made a line across her jaw, ending with her mouth. Her chest rose and fell in short breaths. His tongue traced the line between her lips, and she gasped, opening them. He dipped inside and tasted the sweetness of her. When she fingered the hair at the back of his neck, the throbbing in his breeches threatened to explode.

Kit pulled back and held her close, running his hand along her back. "By God, Grace. I will have you. You cannot deny me." He tipped her head back and kissed her tenderly again. Her head began to shake back and forth, her entire body trembling. But as she locked her gaze on him, it was not fear but anger in her glistening eyes.

"I can't. I can't do this." She pushed away from him, looking around as if lost. "Oh, god. Oh, god. I cannot do this."

Mrs. Whitten hurried into the kitchen. "Here we are. It will just take a moment and we'll have that burn fixed in no time."

Kit saw the panic in Grace's eyes. He wanted to grab her again and shake some sense into her. He tried words instead. "No, cease this nonsense now. I said, I won't allow it."

"My lord, it's just a poultice. I swear to you, it won't hurt you any." The cook clucked at him as she waddled over to the table. "Now here you go... Oh, my lady. What is the matter?" She looked accusingly at Kit.

An agonizing moan ricocheted through the kitchen, and Grace picked her up dress and ran from the room. Mrs. Whitten glared at Kit, and he shrugged his shoulders, his mouth set in an angry line. With a snort, he mumbled, "Thou art not false, but thou art fickle."

Grace dashed up the second flight of stairs, pushed open her door, and slammed it closed. She sank against the hard wood, welcoming the pain against her spine. How could she be such a green girl, a clunch. It had been a simple request and had filled her with joy until uncertainty smothered the rapture, and the sharp taste of self-doubt coated her tongue. The words had stuck in her throat.

The kiss had been so unexpected. And wonderful. And terrifying. His touch, his body, the taste of him consumed her. She was on fire and melting, losing herself in the passion. With horror, she remembered throwing her arms around him like a trollop. She had clung to him and lost all reason when his lips touched hers. A tiny explosion, like gunpowder in the cup, had rocked the careful foundation she had built to protect her future. His passion could convince her to give up everything she held dear. The world that cushioned her from pain and heartache.

She'd escaped to the safety of her room. The protection of a future without love. The safety of loneliness. She cradled her head on her knees and let the tears flow, tension of the last month wash over her, cleanse her. Sunderland had shown her nothing but courtesy and consideration. He was handsome, charming, and kind. Sammy and her father liked him immensely and if she were to make a list, he would check every quality of a perfect match.

A soft knock on the door. "Gracie? It's Eliza. May I come in?"

With a sigh, she rose, wiped her face, and shook out her wrinkled skirt before she opened the door. Eliza entered and hugged her. "Oh my dear, what happened? I saw you racing down the hall as if the devil himself was after you."

"Lord Sunderland wishes to…woo me."

"You cannot be surprised. He is your escort on our daily walks in the garden, your attentive partner in any of the parlor games. His eyes follow you across a room. Did you not expect this?" Eliza's eyebrows drew together. "What aren't you telling me?"

"He kissed me."

Eliza gasped then beamed. "Oh, Grace. How wonderful. That is more than courting. He wants to marry you."

She nodded, the pounding of her heart drowning out her ragged breath.

"What did you tell him?"

Grace could not meet her cousin's eyes. She simply shook her head.

"I pray it was not a harsh cut. He has been through so much with the death of Carson."

Grace clutched her chest. He bared his heart to her, still freshly bruised from the loss of his brother, and she acted as if he were an abhorrent brute. "The kiss was... I couldn't think...and then I panicked. I fled. I saw a husband, and leg shackles, and patronizing looks when I mentioned improvements on the estate and—"

"Grace Beaumont, stop it. How can you know what sort of husband he will make? Has he shown you a domineering nature? Has he been patronizing in any way?"

She shook her head, swiping at her wet cheeks.

"If you knew his mother better, these fears would subside. Meek and obedient are the last words I would use to describe her. As she is the woman who raised him, I cannot imagine he would settle for any less in his own wife. He respects her and loves her." Eliza tipped her cousin's chin with a finger. "But you know that, don't you?"

Grace bobbed her head.

"What is the real reason?"

"I cannot leave Papa and Sammy. I cannot lose the two people who have kept me from drowning these past years. Living without them petrifies me." She ended in a whisper then let out a breath. "It's not my independence I am fighting for. Oh lord, it is what I have been hiding behind."

Her cousin's voice softened. "You've finally realized it."

"You knew?"

"Yes, but it isn't something I could tell you, is it? You would have stomped your foot and denied it until you turned blue." She smiled sadly. "It was something you had to discover on your own."

"I've been such a fool."

"If you refuse a courtship, you will never know what you might have lost. Or gained." Eliza crossed her arms, a stern look sharpening her features. "So what is the plan? You always have a plan."

"I think I owe Lord Sunderland an apology." A teary smile formed, and Grace hugged her best friend. "Thank you."

"It's what friends do. We will always be here for each other. We are family."

Grace never had the chance to offer an apology. Entering the drawing room before dinner, she found Lady Falsbury in tears. Eliza sat next to her, an arm around the older woman. She looked at Grace, concern darkening her violet eyes.

"What is it?" Grace hurried across the room. "Is there anything I can do?"

The marchioness shook her head. "We received a note that Falsbury's carriage overturned. He's hurt but we have no idea what condition he is in." She held a handkerchief to her dark eyes. Grace noticed the circles beneath.

"Your father rode along with Kit so he could return quickly with news."

"Where did it happen?"

"The toll gate south of here," answered Eliza.

"That's only twenty miles away. We'll know soon enough, my lady. I'm sure he's fine." Grace hoped her voice sounded more confident than she felt. This poor family did not need another tragedy so close on the heels of the last.

The cook had left out a cold meat supper for Lord Boldon. The ladies remained in the drawing room and Eliza and Grace continued to keep up Lady Falsbury's spirits. Sammy had gone to bed long ago, tired from a swim in the pond after dinner. The sound of hoofbeats on the drive had all three hurrying from the room. As the butler opened the huge oak door, Grace saw her father dismounting. His great bay gleamed in the lamplight, his coat covered in sweat. The urgency of the ride could mean one of two things. Had he rode like the devil to bring them good news or bad?

He met them in three strides and smiled at the marchioness. "He'll live, my lady. The physician is worried about a cracked ankle and swelling on the knee. But he was fit enough to yell orders to the innkeeper and complain about the price of the carriage."

The proper Lady Falsbury nodded, wiped at the tears spilling from her eyes, and promptly fainted. Eliza screamed as Lord Boldon scooped up the exhausted woman and carried her back into the drawing room. Grace yelled for smelling salts but there was no need.

"Gracious, tell me I didn't swoon." Lady Falsbury leaned her head against the back of the sofa. "I haven't done that since I was a girl. We had that terrible hot summer and I insisted on playing a game of Graces."

"It's been a trying day, my lady." Eliza smoothed the hair from her mother-in-law's forehead. "Take a drink of this cordial."

She smiled and obliged, soon able to sit up on her own. Grace listened with amusement as her father recounted the details of the afternoon.

"It seems some fop had tried to show off his new pair of steppers. Unfortunately, the horses had more experience than he did, and they soon parted company." He shook his head at the folly of youth. "The runaways headed straight for the toll gate, and your husband's driver couldn't move out of the way fast enough. The horses made a sharp turn to avoid Falsbury's team but overturned the phaeton."

"What about the animals?" asked Grace. She hated the thought of a fine animal being sacrificed for some peep-o-day boy.

"I'm happy to report no fatalities today. However," he bowed to his hostess and cringed as he continued. "I'm afraid your new chaise has seen some significant damage. Only one side will open and two wheels need replacing."

She waved her hand. "It's only money. It makes no difference."

"I'm to inform you that your son will remain at the inn until the carriage is repaired and the doctor feels your husband is able to travel. It will be at least several days before they arrive." He looked around the room, his eyes landing on the brandy snifter.

"Oh, goodness. You must be parched. Please, pour yourself a drink then Grace will accompany you to the dining room. There should be some cold meats and cheeses. If you want anything else, please don't hesitate to ask." She smiled at her daughter-in-law. "My dear, would you stay with me a while longer?"

Eliza smiled. "Of course. I'll walk with you to your rooms when you are able."

"I tell you my dear, I don't think my heart can take much more." She cupped Eliza's cheek in her palm. "I thank the heavens above when you were sent to me. What would I do without you?"

Eliza's back was to Grace but she heard her mumbling and watched her cousin fuss over the woman. She realized, as she quietly shut the door, that Eliza had found a loving family. She had married Carson as an outsider, but somehow his death had provided a place for Eliza in the Falsbury household. The two women were devoted to each other and the strong affection was apparent. A line from one of Lord Milton's poems came to mind:

Was I deceived, or did a sable cloud
Turn forth her silver lining on the night?

Milton's sable clouds had certainly found a silver lining for Eliza.

"You pierce my soul. I am half agony, half hope."

Jane Austen *Persuasion*

Chapter Fourteen

August 1815
Boldon Estate

They had returned to Boldon over two weeks ago. Lord Falsbury had been unable to travel for almost a week, so there had been no opportunity to apologize to Lord Sunderland. He'd preoccupied her thoughts ever since. She passed several men clipping the lawn. Their long scythes swung in smooth, practiced strokes. Grace watched for a moment, losing herself in the soft beat, listening to the *swish, swish* of the blades slicing the clover. Life had fallen into its usual rhythm but Grace was unsettled. Daily tasks that had once given her pleasure were now a chore. The days stretched in front of her like an endless desert, no relief in sight. Nothing had changed. Everything had changed.

She walked toward the herb plot, breathing in the earthy scent of soil and floral, pungent and sweet. White cabbage and lettuces were abundant, rounded heads and broad leaves creating a light and dark green patchwork against the stone wall. Purple cabbage, used for pickling, added a lovely color to the section. Sammy's favorite, the asparagus, was already dying out. The gardens encompassed several acres now and continued to expand.

It had taken much persuasion to convince Papa to build another greenhouse. When she had seen her father bending, she had played her trump card. He would have fresh cucumbers in January. Oh, how Papa loved cucumbers. The two stone buildings faced the north so the remaining three walls maintained exposure to the sun. The expensive rows of glass, encased between the red-brown brick, flashed in the afternoon light. The older building would house the tender plants that could not withstand the English winters. The second building would soon boast heat, and more work for a local gardener. The boiler had to be kept going throughout the long, cold months.

Continuing down the path, she stopped to snip some chamomile. Papa was breaking in a new horse. The herb placed in a hot bath would ease his sore muscles. She absently rubbed a stem of rosemary and held it to her nose.

Rosemary is for remembrance,
Between us day and night.
Wishing that I may always,
Have you present in my sight.

What must he think of her? How could she face him again? And why did his opinion worry her so? The accident had been fortuitous; she had not fled the Falsbury Castle to avoid him. Yet, she found his view of her was vital to her happiness. That made her grit her teeth. Independent women did not measure their contentment by a man's attention.

She had avoided marriage for several years. So, the whole situation had worked out rather well. But her mind continued to play back scenes from the past month. His devilish grin, his antics with Sammy, the teasing and games in the evening. The last day together haunted when she closed her eyes. Her body betrayed her then, waking in a sweat, panting from the kiss he could never have given her at the castle. Papa watched her, a question in his eyes. He knew what she did not want to admit.

"And when I cannot have
As I have said before,
Then Cupid, with his deadly dart,
Doth wound my heart full sore."

She loved him, with every muscle in her body, every breath in her lungs, every thought in her muddled mind.

Oh god help me, I love him, she whispered.

Is this how her mother had felt? The desperate, mad rush of desire, the trembling of her body, the racing of her heart when those dark eyes took her in from slipper to smile. She missed that crooked grin when he and Sammy played some foolish game and tried to pull her into it. His voice would come back to her in a familiar phrase or remembered conversation.

"My lady."

She jumped and turned too quickly, putting her hand out for balance. Mr. Chenwick looked aghast.

"I did not mean to startle you, Lady Grace. You have a visitor and your father has not returned from his ride yet. He is in the library."

"Who?" She struggled to bring her mind back to the present.

"A Lord Sunderland, my lady. Where shall I have him wait?"

Do not panic, her brain scolded. *Composure, calm.*

"Please instruct the butler to have him wait in the drawing room. Could you also have Master Samuel join us there?"

The thin, graying tutor hastened back to the mansion. Grace clutched the chamomile, crushing the delicate white flowers and followed at a sedate pace. *Deep breath*, she told herself, *deep breath*. She pulled her gloves off, handed the napkin of herbs to Mrs. Woolley, and removed her bonnet. "Could you make some tea, please? I shall be in the drawing room with our guest. Sammy will be joining us and I..."

Mrs. Woolley looked at her expectantly. "Yes, my lady?"

"Could you please remain in the room until my father returns or our guest leaves?"

"Of course, I'll bring the tea straight away."

Kit paced the room but stopped at a portrait of who could only be Lady Boldon. Her daughter had the same intelligent eyes and shining auburn hair. They might have been sisters. It must have been hard for Lord Boldon to see his wife's younger image after her death. He remembered how difficult it had been for Eliza when he had arrived at Falsbury. Oh, he had missed this family. Several times, an antic of Sammy's would cross his mind and a laugh would burst from him. He had been rehearsing this speech under his breath for a week. His valet was beginning to think he was headed for Bedlam.

In London, Weston had recognized how unsettled he'd been and invited him to the Wicked Earls' Club for some distraction. Kit's frustration at how things had been left between Grace and him had frayed his nerves. His newfound friends had all seemed to know the perfect remedy. They promised a night of gambling, drink, and a woman to bed, in particular, to rid him of the tension he could not shake. Coventry had smiled in understanding and set him up in Carson's old chambers, in case the night was a bit more than the earl had anticipated. It was as if his brother's old devil had hovered over him in the club. Kit had drunk too much port, lost too much in whist, and then headed up to the room to sleep it off. Overindulging was not his style, and he didn't want anyone seeing him in such a condition. But entering the room, he'd found a lovely lady-bird in the bed, soft and feminine, blonde and buxom. Exactly the type he'd always enjoyed in the past.

The girl had been willing, tasted of honey, with hands that knew how to please a man. But instead of a much-needed release, Grace's face appeared behind his closed lids. Her sweet smile, those luminous emerald eyes, that slender body that would fit his like a puzzle piece. Sex had always been part of a regiment to keep his mind and body fit. But now his mind and heart was at odds with the rest of him. He'd ordered the girl from the room with a handful of coins. The lightskirt had apologized, not understanding his rejection. With Carson's ghost still haunting him, Kit went on the cut and got foxed. Thank god for Weston. He didn't remember how he got home, vaguely remembered Andrew guiding him down the club's back stairs. The next morning he made plans to visit Boldon Estate.

The door opened and she was there, the sun creating streaks of fire through her chestnut curls. "Lady Grace," he bowed, cringing at the crack in his voice. Not a good beginning.

"Good day, Lord Sunderland. What an unexpected surprise."

She sounded breathless. He felt his body stir. When she licked her lips, he almost came undone. "It seems I own a castle nearby, and the estate manager has decided to retire."

"Oh, the haunted castle, yes. So you've been there?" She smiled and sat in a chair by the window. "Won't you take a seat?"

He lifted his tails and settled across from her. "As in ghosts? And no, I came here first."

"Yes. There are half a dozen legends about the place. I remember walking past it once with my governess. Such eerie sounds came from the place. As a girl, I was petrified. Now, I'm sure it was only the wind." She grinned. "I'm sure you'll be fine."

"Thank you, I... Well, I..." He closed his eyes. *You can charge into a battle, outnumbered two to one, and you can't say three little words to this woman.* He opened his eyes, determined to maintain his dignity, when Sammy burst into the room.

"Sunderland, you came to see me. I knew you'd miss us. I told Gracie." He skidded to a stop, wrinkling the Axminster carpet beneath his boots. The boy stomped his feet and smoothed out the rug. He also noted that the housekeeper was hovering in a far corner. Good, they couldn't be accused of anything inappropriate. "Will you stay for dinner?"

"Sammy, it's not your place to invite Lord Sunderland. I'm sure he has business to attend at his castle." She tilted her head and gave her brother some type of look that Kit didn't recognize and the boy ignored.

"Papa will ask him anyway. It's only polite." He moved between Grace's knees and leaned back against her. "How is your father? Is his leg fixed?"

"He's making an excellent recovery. I thank you for asking."

"You have to stay because I have so many things to show you. The lake, my pony, the swing Papa put up in the oak tree." He paused. "The *haunted* castle?"

The maid entered with the tea at that moment. Sammy hopped up and down beside her, trying to see which biscuits had been set out. Grace scolded him again. "I am sorry, my lord, he is quite active today."

She poured the tea, an image of aristocratic grace, and he wished they were alone. He needed privacy, and the words he'd practiced were for her ears only. As he reached for the cup, Sammy leapt over his arm to snatch a biscuit. The tea crashed to the floor, splattering across the boy's shirt and the carpet.

"Samuel! Where are your manners?" Grace took the biscuit from him, her lips pressed together. "Mrs. Woolley?"

"I've got him, my lady." The housekeeper took Samuel by the hand and led him from the room. "And I'll send the maid in to clean up the mess."

Kit looked at the frustration in Grace's eyes. "Well, we aren't off to a good start, are we?" He laughed. The tension was gone. "Shall we stay here alone without a chaperone? Or take a walk on the lawn with several fellows clipping and at attention?"

Grace giggled. "I choose the walk."

Kit rose and followed her to the door. As they walked along the front of the mansion, he folded his hands behind his back. "I'm afraid we left things rather unsettled at Falsbury. I was disappointed to find you had gone."

She nodded. "We stayed as long as possible but Papa had appointments he could not postpone. You know, he was only planning on staying a week."

"Really? What changed his mind?"

"The company, I presume. He said he hadn't enjoyed himself so much since my mother died." She peeked at him from the corner of her eye. "Thank you. It was a generous invitation. We all had a lovely visit."

"Will you come to London?" He noticed her hesitate at the question. "Lady Eliza will be disappointed if you are not there for the birth of her child."

"Oh, yes. We are planning to come late November since she is due in early December. It was arranged with your mother before we left." Grace smiled at him, mischief sparkling in her eyes. "In fact, we convinced Eliza to allow Lady Falsbury to secure the services of Sir William Knighton."

"The physician who specializes in childbirth?" Kit knew the man had attended members of the royal family. He would charge no small commission. The fact his mother was so involved in the birth of her grandchild, and taking on the cost, told him how much she cared for Eliza.

"Will you return to the military if she has a boy?" Grace asked, her head turned toward the men. "My father said it was your preference."

"It was."

"Was? Has something changed?"

"You came along, my lady." He stopped, admiring her profile as she continued for a few steps. Realizing he was no longer beside her, she paused. "I believe we need to continue the conversation we began at Falsbury. I'm afraid I made a mull of it."

"Oh no! It was my fault. An unreasonable mistrust that made me run rather than speak my mind. It's not characteristic of me, I assure you." She held her head up, her chin out. "I am not a coward by nature."

"I don't think anything of the kind. Lady Grace, I am not a man who would appreciate leg-shackles in marriage. In turn, I would not attach them to my wife. You fear that marriage will put you under a man's thumb."

She nodded, an embarrassed smile curling her plump lips.

"We've talked about your upbringing by an independent mother and a tolerant father. I commend you on the raising of your brother thus far. *My* mother is not one to stifle her opinions either, so I am not accustomed to a meek or silly woman."

Lady Grace shook her head. "It was the kiss... I'd never experienced such feelings. My resolve melted away, and I was afraid."

"Of me? Of us?" His pulse beat in his neck. It was time to tread softly regardless of the ardor turning him rigid.

"I am afraid of leaving my family." Her eyes held his, a steady but pleading gaze.

"Of course you are. How could you not? You have been companion, daughter, mother, and sister for five years. Most women would never have given up so much for their family. But I would not choose such a female to be *my* wife."

Her chest rose and fell, the cream lace tracing her bosom, the movement sending ripples down the deep blue muslin. "What are you saying?"

Kit put his finger under her chin and lifted her face, careful to keep the other hand behind his back. He didn't trust himself at this moment. "I love you. I have not had a moment's peace since you left. No, since we met on the hill overlooking Falsbury. You invaded my soul that day. And the weeks after, you unlocked my heart. Tell me I have not been misguided in my affection." There. He had laid bare his soul. It was his ace in the hand.

"Lord Sunderland, I am a silly rattleplate. I ran from you that day because I realized how much I cared for you. During the play, being so close to you, my body understood my feelings before I did." She clasped her hands together. "I'm not as sophisticated as the ladies in your circle. My place has always been here at Boldon. The ways of courting and flirtation are foreign to me. But I have listened to my heart, and it spoke to me after your kiss."

"And what does your heart tell you?"

"You are a fine man, and any woman would be fortunate to have your affection."

He let out a breath. "I want to marry you. I want to be with you. I want to love you until you are breathless and swoon from it. And if I don't kiss you soon, I'm certain I will die from it."

Her eyes glittered and an impish smile slanted across her face. "We mustn't have that."

Oh, she was tempting. He wanted to crush her to him and devour her mouth, taste her, inhale her.

He blew out another breath instead and chuckled. "You are a vixen, Lady Grace."

He bent and lightly brushed his lips across hers. She shivered under his touch. He smiled as he stepped back.

"And you are a rake, Lord Sunderland." The humor faded from her eyes. "I love you, but I don't know if I can leave Boldon, my father and brother. What if I am miserable? What if I make you unhappy? What if I disappoint you—"

His mouth came down on hers again, more demanding this time to silence her doubts. He buried his fingers in her hair, the strands like silk against his calloused skin. Her palms rested on his chest, her body curving against him.

The men on the lawn cheered. Grace covered her face with her hands, hiding the blush he knew spread over her cheeks. She ducked her head, her chest heaving.

"I apologize, my lady, but this is what you have driven me to." Her dazed expression, the swollen lips gripped him with a passion he'd only known before battle. He understood now why a man would allow his wife to follow him in war. "The only way you could disappoint me is to say no. Lady Grace, make me the happiest of men and be my wife."

She lifted her head, her mouth still parted. Her tongue ran across her top lip and she took a deep breath. "Yes, but—" He put a finger to her lips.

"I have taken your concerns into consideration." He grinned as he threw her own words back at her. "And I have a *plan*."

"Children are the anchors that hold a mother to life."

Sophocles

Chapter Fifteen

Late November 1815
London, England

That was demmed fast. I knew you were interested in her, but didn't realize... By God, we just gave you a key a few months ago." Weston slapped him on the back. "To most men I would offer my sympathy, but this chit had you back to your old self before summer had gone. "

Kit grinned. "Lord Boldon arrives at his townhouse later this week. You'll meet her then. She's coming for the birth of my niece or nephew."

"So the plans are all in order?"

"Yes, nothing has changed. Falsbury prefers I don't return to my military career. If it's a boy, he wants me to assume guardianship. Says he's too old to worry about another youngster. Regardless of the outcome, we will reside at Sunderland Castle. If I want to spend any time with my wife, we need to live near her family estate." He ran a hand through his hair. "The grounds need major repairs. I've managed to make one wing livable, so we can reside there while renovations are underway."

"We'll need to kick over the traces at the Wicked Earls' Club before you sign the marriage contract."

"Several times, I hope. The company and gaming are excellent there, but I won't need any more doxies in my room."

"I promise it will be a bit more tame than Carson's excursions."

A silence settled between them, each lost in a memory.

Grace checked her reflection for the third time before joining her father at the door. In less than an hour, she would see Kit and Eliza again. She had not seen her cousin since late September. Papa had been invited to hunt partridge at Lady Rafferton's estate, and they had stayed at Falsbury for the week. Kit had been busy getting Sunderland Castle habitable again, so he had split his time between inspecting various properties with his father, working on the crumbling castle, and London. Still, it had been a month since her heart had raced when he entered a room.

She pulled a ringlet in front of her ear, adjusted the wide green ribbon in her hair, and smoothed out the velvet of her emerald green dress. Two bands of deep purple, embroidered with gold thread in Celtic swirls, ran down each side of her skirt. A matching embroidered ribbon wrapped around her waist. Yanking her gloves up to her elbows, she smiled at herself and pinched her cheeks. *Oh gracious*, she thought, *he loves you as you are, stop fussing*. As she descended the stairs, her purple slippers peeked out from the hem.

"You are a beauty, my dear." Her father beamed. "This will be a grand visit."

"I only wish Sammy was here with us." She hated the whine in her voice.

"We discussed this. You must adapt to his absence. We shall only be gone a week or two until the babe arrives." He patted her shoulder with a chuckle. "This too, we shall survive."

"I know, Papa. It's my first time away from him, that's all." Stretching on her tiptoes, she kissed his cheek. "I will be happy to see Eliza and concentrate on that."

"Only Eliza?" His bushy brows rose. "Someone else may have been on your mind when you dressed tonight. A new gown?"

She bit her lip. "Yes, but I—"

"No need to explain. You rarely spend a coin on yourself." He kissed her back on the top of her head.

The carriage pulled up to the front steps. The lady's maid helped her on with the golden brown pelisse; the plush fox of the collar and cuffs feathered her skin as she drew it around her. Grace tucked her reticule inside the large fur muff then took her father's elbow. The ride to the Falsbury townhouse was short. The street lamps had already been lit, and snow had begun to fall. In the glow of oil lights, snowflakes danced and twisted to the ground, covering the grime of the city in a pristine white blanket.

"Are you warm enough, my dear?"

"Oh, yes Papa." She rubbed her feet against the hot wrapped bricks. "Did you know Eliza plans to stay with Lady Falsbury regardless if she has a boy or girl?"

He nodded. "Strange how things have worked out. The marchioness has become more of a maternal figure to the girl than her own mother. Not that I blame your aunt in any way. She is a victim of circumstance."

Grace said a silent prayer for all women in such circumstances. The carriage rolled onto the crescent, and stopped at the center residence of the terrace. The arc-shaped row of townhouses was lit with fan lights over each door. Falsbury's lamp illuminated the white pilasters flanking either side of the entrance and the pineapple frieze above the door that welcomed visitors. It stood four stories tall, miniature wrought-iron balconies adorning the middle rows of windows. In the summer, the attached flower boxes would hold summer blooms.

The butler ushered them in and soon they were in the drawing room. Eliza tried to bound from the chair, fell back, and pushed herself forward again. Sunderland was at her elbow in a moment, escorting her across the room.

Grace met them in the middle, her arms going around her cousin but her eyes on Kit. The wings in her stomach awoke, provoked by the warm, secret smile he sent her way. The smile that said, *I've missed you. I long to hold you in my arms.*

"Gracie, it's so good to see you," cried Eliza, wiping at her eyes then laughing at her look of concern. "Don't mind me. I seem to burst into tears these days over trifles. Doesn't matter if I'm happy, angry, sad, or just bored."

"I was worse off than you," chimed in Lady Falsbury with a flap of hand, dismissing her daughter-in-law's outburst. Kit's mother was glowing in a print of dusty rose with scalloped lace at the throat and sleeves. "Don't go trotting too much, my dear. We don't want that baby coming early."

Kit bowed low over Grace's hand, winking at her as his lips lingered on her gloved hand. Her pulse quickened in anticipation of a stolen moment later in the evening. They were engaged after all and Eliza had assured her no outsiders had been invited.

At dinner, Kit threw protocol to the wind and sat next to his fiancée. It had been over a month, and if he couldn't pull her off to a dark corner, he would at least sit beside her. The women had talked incessantly of the upcoming birth. He'd learned more than he needed to know about Sir William Knighton, the accoucheur attending the birth, the monthly nurse now in residence, the "lowering" diet Eliza was on that restricted the intake alcohol, tea or coffee, and the birthing room. Finally, the meal would provide alternative subjects.

"Have you been to Tattersall's of late, Sunderland?" asked Boldon, a twinkle in his brown eyes. "I'm considering breeding my best carriage horse. I'll need to replace her if I do. Would you like to take a look at the stock tomorrow?"

"Could we discuss something other than procreation?" Kit gave him a sullen side-glance and was rewarded with a hearty chuckle.

"I'm just kicking up a lark," he replied with good humor. "We'll have our port soon enough and the ladies may continue their delicate talk."

"I haven't heard a delicate word since they began," he mumbled under his breath. It must have been loud enough for Grace to hear because she pinched him under the table. "Ouch! You'll pay for that," he warned in a loud whisper. She giggled and her scent of vanilla and...orange filled his nose. When desire stirred his loins, he reluctantly went back to thoughts of the accoucheur.

The subject of Christmas and social events vied with pregnancy the rest of the meal. He noted Eliza looked pale this evening. Even though his mother had reminded her meat and rich dishes should be avoided this late in her pregnancy, but fish was an excellent choice. She had only sipped at the white soup and partaken in none of the corner dishes of fish. *Are all women so preoccupied with such details?* he wondered. A plan to ban his mother and Eliza from Sunderland Castle during Grace's confinement began to form.

The remove dishes were replaced and the second course began. He served himself and Grace a portion of roasted filet of pork and lamb chop sautéed with asparagus and peas.

"I will excuse myself just before you retire to the drawing room. Find a reason to delay, so you leave the dining room alone," he said quietly, sticking his fork into a chunk of pork covered in a rich brown sauce. He moved his knee and brushed the velvet of her dress, watching Grace's eyes widen and press her lips together.

But as the second course removes were taken away, an uproar began at the end of the table. "Are you sure?" asked his mother in a high-pitched voice. Sir Knighton is out of town. It cannot happen until next week at the earliest."

Eliza pushed back her chair and bent low, clutching her belly. "You had better tell your grandchild because she isn't listening."

"My grandson seems to be as contrary as his father," mumbled Lady Falsbury. "Gentlemen, I'm afraid you'll have to finish the meal without us." She stood and leaned over Eliza. "Come my dear, let's get you upstairs."

Grace shot up from her chair, toppling it backward. Kit caught it before it hit the floor. "Are you well?" he asked, concern over the sudden paleness of her skin.

"Grace..." Her father's words were calm and soothing. "It will be fine. The monthly nurse is here. I am sure Lady Falsbury found the best in London."

"Certainly, nothing less for my grandson."

"Granddaughter," corrected Eliza.

"We'll soon see," grinned Kit. He was disappointed his private moment with Grace would be forfeited, but the mystery would finally be solved. "Please, let me assist the lady to her room."

It took a quarter of an hour to reach the lying-in room on the third floor. Another contraction had rippled over Eliza, and she'd sat on a stair, panting. Her cousin's earlier alarm had vanished, and she'd held the girl's hand until the pain subsided.

"I've had small pains all day, but I didn't think it was worth mentioning. The last time, Sir Knighton said it was a false start out of the gate." She began to laugh but the sound turned into a moan as she lumbered to her feet. "I might have misjudged."

Kit lost his patience. "Lady Eliza, I don't want to cause you duress, but please let me carry you the rest of the way."

He had expected an argument. Instead, her eyes filled with gratitude as she nodded her consent. She was lighter than he expected. He scooped her up into his arms, the other women following close behind.

They had chosen chambers that would provide morning light for the mother and child. There was a large bedroom, dressing room, and an outer chamber, Kit assumed, for anyone waiting to hear news. He would happily wait downstairs with Boldon and drink port.

He gently deposited Lady Eliza on the bed, kissed Grace on top of the head while his mother arranged the sheets, and escaped. In the dining room, Boldon had foregone the last courses and poured two glasses of port.

"To a new generation," he toasted, handing Kit a glass of the dark liquid.

"I'll be happy when this is over. Grace and I will set a date, be married, and begin our own family." He was anxious to get started with this new phase of his life. The optimism that greeted him in the mirror each day was the result of this newfound tenderness. The abyss left by Carson's death was shrinking with Grace's love. She filled it, filled him with hope that the world could be a good place with laughter and family. This birth would make her hungry for a child. He was ready. At long last, he was ready and had Grace to thank for this new view of the future.

By midnight, Kit was pacing the floor. They had moved to the billiard room to keep busy. Boldon had gone up once and came back, shaking his head. "Not yet, not yet. These things take time. One never knows."

Foreboding churned in his gut. "What is it?"

"The baby is turned sideways."

"Well, they can straighten it out. Can't they?"

"I don't know." Boldon's mouth tightened. "The nurse is afraid to intervene without Sir Knighton.

She's afraid if something goes wrong, she will be blamed."

Kit ran a hand through his hair and began to pace. "Is there nothing we can do?"

"Wait. And have another drink."

Two hours later, a rap sounded at the door. A servant curtsied and announced, "You are needed upstairs, my lord."

They dropped their cue sticks and headed toward the door. "Lord Boldon, my lords."

Kit ignored the maid, and both men continued down the hall, taking the stairs two at a time. Hesitating at the entrance of the outer chamber, he heard a low moan of despair. "No-o-o, no, no." Fear skittered down his spine as his mother emerged from the room.

"She was like a general in battle. The nurse was afraid to turn the baby, and Eliza was tiring. Lady Grace pushed up her sleeves, and pulled the nurse back to the bed. She said they would both die if nothing was done, and she wouldn't allow that to happen." Lady Falsbury sat down with a sigh. The lines in her face had deepened in the last few hours. "With Grace's assistance, the nurse was able to turn the child. As they delivered her into the world, the usual fluids came rushing out, mixed with blood. It's perfectly normal, but when Eliza went limp and the baby was not breathing, Grace panicked."

"And Eliza?" asked Lord Boldon.

"She's weak but will recover. However, I think between the blood and the child not breathing immediately, it brought back memories of your wife. Her body began to tremble, and she backed away from the bed, calling for her mother. I tried to reassure her then removed her from the room."

Another quiet sob from the back of the chamber. "I can't reach her, Lord Boldon. I thought perhaps if you tried, we could calm her enough to see that everyone is fine. I'm afraid Grace is locked in her past..."

Kit had heard enough. Anger made him push past the door with force. It banged against the wall, startling the occupants. Through the open frame, he saw Eliza propped up in the bed, a bundle in her arms and a woman tending to them both.

"Please, my lord. We do not need any more commotion." The nurse returned her attention to her patient, sponging the sweat from her face.

With a weak smile, Eliza turned to him. "You have a niece, *Lord Sunderland.* And I have Grace to thank for her safe delivery. Please, help her."

He heard a hiccup and a long intake a breath. Then he saw her. Huddled in the corner, her knees drawn up, and her head buried in her arms. Kit approached her slowly, squatted down, and smoothed back the wet tendrils curled on her cheek. "Grace, my love, I'm here."

"Why, Mama? Why again?" Her glazed eyes were puffy, her tear-streaked cheeks red. She couldn't see him, her mind was back at Boldon five years ago. The sight of her pierced his heart. His beautiful, confident, infuriating, beloved Grace. *Oh god*, his mind screamed, *not now. Not when we're so close to a life together*.

Kit placed his hands beneath her with care, as if she might break if he moved too quickly, and lifted her into his arms. He held her to his chest, tucking her head beneath his chin, whispering to her as he carried her out of the room. "Shh, shh my love. I'm here now, shh."

Her father stood at the door, his eyes shining with concern. "Oh, my poor little girl." He looked at Lady Falsbury, his eyes shining and his voice thick. "Will she come back to us?"

Kit saw his mother guide Boldon from the room. "On second thought, I think if anyone can reach her now, it will be my son. From what Eliza has told me, she needs a voice from her future not her past, to pull her from this dark place."

Grace began to cry again, a soft, heart-wrenching sound that threatened to shred Kit's very soul. He sat down against the sofa, rocking her, whispering words of love, kissing her hair. "Shh, I'm here, my sweet. Eliza and the baby need you now. Sammy is waiting for you. It's time to come home."

A strangled groan echoed in his ears, and he continued to rock her. She couldn't break down now. Not now, when he was whole again. Not now, when his life was filled with light and laughter. Not now, when her smile helped him heal a little more each day.

"By God, Grace, I won't allow it. Come back to me, dammit. Blast them all, *I* need you." He buried his face in her neck, his tears mixing with hers, and realized the tormented groan was his. "I *need* you."

A hand stroked his hair, a whispered touch. Fingers curved around his neck. "Kit?" It was a raspy sound, hoarse and barely audible. The most beautiful sound he'd ever heard.

He let out a long, unsteady breath. "Grace, I'm here my darling." He clutched her to him, rocking and laughing and kissing her eyes, cheeks, nose, lips. "I'll always be right here."

"I saw the blood then Eliza wasn't responding, and the baby was so still..."

"Mother and daughter are fine." He considered setting her in a chair so he could fetch a cool cloth and some water for her. His mind said to release her; his heart wouldn't let her go.

"It's a girl? They're both alive?"

"You saved them, my stubborn, fearless little chit."

Her hand cupped his cheek, and he leaned into it. "No, you are the hero. I heard you scolding me. I felt your tears and wanted to wipe them away. Kit, my love, you saved *me*, by chasing away the darkness that's been hiding in my heart for so long."

Grace lifted her head and pressed her lips to his. He closed his eyes, understood the silent promise in the kiss, and his world began to turn again.

"Be thou the rainbow in the storms of life. The evening beam that smiles the clouds away, and tints tomorrow with prophetic ray."

Lord Byron

Epilogue

Early December 1815

Grace swayed back and forth, soaking up the baby's warmth, inhaling the sweet infant scent. The embarrassment of last week had faded. The tenderness for her future husband had grown tenfold. She hadn't realized the horror of childbirth and death had haunted her, made a home in her soul. When the baby came, she had spiraled down into the depths of those fears, sinking into a shadowy pit, reliving her mother's death. Kit had brought her back; his voice had penetrated the fog. She had reached for him, and he'd pulled her up, held her close, wouldn't let her go. He would keep the darkness at bay, always. Her heart swelled, remembering how his words had gone from soft and soothing to angry and demanding. He loved her. Oh, how he loved her.

Kit tickled the little girl's chin. "Hello, Althea, you gave us quite a scare."

Lady Falsbury fussed over Eliza, smoothing her bedsheets again. "The nurse said we can open the window for a bit of fresh air. Not too long, I don't want either of you to catch a chill. Your diet should remain—"

"Mother, stop fretting over the woman and come hold your granddaughter," Kit ordered. "It's been almost a week and you've repeated the accoucheur's orders so many times, I can recite them by heart."

With a glare, his mother took the child from Grace. "Come here, my little one. We waited such a long time for you. Your grandfather will be furious when he comes home."

"Because it's not a boy?" asked Grace, indignant at the thought the marquess wasn't satisfied with his own son.

"Goodness, no. He's relieved it's a girl, says Christopher always had a mind for business." She cooed at the baby. "Lord Falsbury planned on being here for the birth. He likes to be at the helm for any important event. This certainly qualifies."

"Ha! That will irritate him."

"Eliza, I thought you had chosen Cara for a girl?"

"I had. One day, I was reading a book in the library and came across Althea. It means 'of healing power' and thought it fitting."

"I've never been a philosopher but my brother has accomplished several good deeds in the wake of his death." Kit pulled Grace close. "By marrying Eliza, he provided a safe and happy home for a good woman, my mother with a daughter and a grandchild, and me with a wife. He must be particularly smug right now."

"I hadn't thought of it in that sense. You're right, he's left behind quite a legacy." Eliza gave a wistful smile.

He looked at the ceiling and grinned. "Well Carson, who'd have thought you'd come through in the end?"

Kit swore the warm breath of laughter brushed the back of his head.

Author's Note

Authenticity is very important to me. In every story I write, there are real places, people, and things that exist. In this book, the toy theaters were very popular during the Regency. The play that Sammy put on was a favorite with the boys because of the explosion at the end. Check it out!

https://janeaustensworld.wordpress.com/tag/toy-theatres/

The first male midwives, *accoucheurs*, were growing in popularity. These were educated men who saw the financial gain in this new field. Two well respected and costly obstetricians served London aristocracy and the royal family. Sir William Knighton and Sir Richard Croft.

Sunderland is an area in northern England and was once a bustling port. I came across it when I wrote my medieval story, Rolf's Quest. The villain in that story is Kit's ancestor, who owned Sunderland Castle. You'll meet the mad duke (from Rolf's Quest) when Kit and Grace move in to the haunted castle. But you'll have to wait until Christmas 2018.

Eliza's story, *A Wicked Earl's Widow* begins the *Once Upon A Widow* series releasing summer of 2018. The second book in that series, *Rhapsody and Rebellion* releases October 2018.

Sign up for my newsletter and don't miss future releases.

https://www.subscribepage.com/k3f1z5

Reviews are an author's life blood. If you enjoyed this story, please consider leaving a review for my book on your favorite retailer. Mention that you purchased a paperback copy.

The Wicked Earl's Widow
Once Upon A Widow, Book 1

When Eliza's abusive father forced her into marriage, she had no idea her life would change for the better. Married less than a year, her unwilling rake of a husband had been surprisingly kind to her—until his sudden death. The widowed Countess of Sunderland is more than happy to remain with her in-laws and raise their daughter. Unfortunately, her own family is on the brink of financial ruin and has other plans.

Nathaniel, Viscount of Pendleton, gained his title at the age of 12. His kindly but astute estate manager became father and mentor, instilling in the boy an astute sense of responsibility and compassion for his tenants. Fifteen years later, his family urges him to visit London and seek a wife. The ideal doesn't appeal to him, but his sense of duty tells him it is the next logical step.

When Lord Pendleton stumbles upon Eliza on the road, defending an elderly woman against ruffians, he's shocked and intrigued. After rescuing the exquisite damsel in distress, he finds himself smitten. But Nate soon realizes he must discover the dark secrets of her past to truly save the woman he loves.

Now available on all major retail sites.

About the Author

Bestselling and award-winning author Aubrey Wynne resides in the Midwest with her husband, dogs, horses, mule and barn cats. She is an elementary teacher by trade, champion of children and animals by conscience, and author by night. Obsessions include history, travel, trail riding and all things Christmas.

Her short stories, ***Merry Christmas, Henry and Pete's Mighty Purty Privies*** have won Readers Choice Awards. ***Dante's Gift*** and ***Paper Love*** received the 2016 Golden Quill, Aspen Gold, Heart of Excellence and the Gayle Wilson Award of Excellence.

In addition to her Chicago Christmas novellas, Aubrey will release two more Regency romances in 2018. The Wicked Earls' Club will release again in 2019. Wynne's medieval fantasy series launched in 2017 with ***Rolf's Quest***, winner of the NTRWA Great Expectations.

Also by Aubrey Wynne

Rolf's Quest (A Medieval Encounter #1)
http://aubreywynne.com/aubreys-books/aubreys-historical-romance/
Great Expectations winner, Fire & Ice finalist

"Author Aubrey Wynne brings a swashbuckling epic story of family, love and betrayal to life in "Rolf's Quest". The structure of the story is done well -- it is long on action and moves at breakneck speed. The plot is perfectly paced, with characters that will pull the reader right into the action. They are likable and readers will root for Rolf and Melissa throughout their struggles. The strength of their bond will keep readers glued to their seat right until the very last page. Hold onto your helmet, readers, and grab a shield -- Rolf is just around the corner."

InD'tale magazine

"This was a surprisingly smooth read that I flew through in practically one sitting. I loved how easily I was immersed in this medieval world filled with royalty, knights, wizards, and villains. The magical element was interesting and I liked the way Merlin's story was woven into this book. The plot sucked me in and I thoroughly enjoyed following Rolf's journey.

In closing... A story with pretty much everything a fantasy romance fan can want. 4.5 stars"

Romance Reviews

A wizard, a curse, a fated love...

When Rolf finally discovers the woman who can end the curse that has plagued his family for centuries, she is already betrothed. Time is running out for the royal wizard of King Henry II. If he cannot find true love without the use of sorcery, the magic will die for future generations.

Melissa is intrigued by the mystical, handsome man who haunts her by night and tempts her by day. His bizarre tale of Merlin, enchantments, and finding genuine love has her questioning his sanity and her heart.

From the moment Melissa stepped from his dreams and into his arms, Rolf knew she was his destiny. Now, he will battle against time, a powerful duke, and call on the gods to save her.

Small Town Romance series

Saving Grace (A Small Town Romance #1)

http://aubreywynne.com/smalltown-romance/

"This unique piece has the reader traveling between the early 1700s and the early 2000s with ease and amazement. The audience truly feels sorrow for Grace and Chloe and is able to connect with each woman for the hardships they are overcoming. The attention to historical facts and details leave one breathless especially upon learning the people from the past did exist and the memorial erected still stands."

InD'Tale Magazine

"I enjoyed the way the book went from past to present really pulling the read in. The mystery was a delight. The author gives a wonderful story of two women fighting to keep what is theirs, showing their strength, love and courage to put one foot in front of the other while the world around them goes crazy."

Cyn, Top 500 Reviewer

A tortured soul meets a shattered heart...

Chloe Hicks' life consisted of an egocentric ex-husband, a pile of bills, and an equine business in foreclosure until a fire destroys the stable and her beloved ranch horse. What little hope she has left is smashed after the marshal suspects arson. She escapes the accusing eyes of her hometown, but not the memories and melancholy.

Jackson Hahn, Virginia Beach's local historian, has his eyes on the mysterious new woman in town. When she enters his office, he is struck by her haunting beauty and the raw pain in her eyes. Her descriptions of the odd events happening in her bungalow pique his curiosity.

The sexy historian distracts Chloe with the legend of a woman wrongly accused of witchcraft. She is drawn to the story and the similarities of events that plagued their lives. Perhaps the past can help heal the present. But danger lurks in the shadows...

Just A Girl Next Door (Small Town Romance #2)

"Beautifully written and tells a story that will allow readers to experience the turmoil that war can bring to the lives of those who must endure its heartbreak."

Amazon Review

"This isn't your typical boy-meets-girl-they-get-married-and-live-happily-ever-after-the-end story. This is sweet romance in the midst of real life hardships and pain, and a love that will press through and triumph."

Amazon Review

The Korean War destroyed their plans, but the battle at home may shatter their hearts...

Laura Beth Walters fell in love with Joe McCall when she was six years old. Now she is counting the days until Joey graduates from college so they can marry and begin their life together. But the Korean War rips their neatly laid plans to shreds. Instead of a college fraternity, Joey joins a platoon. Laura Beth trades a traditional wedding for a quick trip to the courthouse.

They endure the hardship of separation, but the true battle is faced when Joey returns from the war. Their marriage is soon tested beyond endurance. Joe and Laura Beth must find a way to accept the trials thrown in their path or lose the love that has kept them anchored for so long.

A Chicago Christmas series

Dante's Gift (A Chicago Christmas #1)

http://aubreywynne.com/book/dantes-gift-a-chicago-christmas-1/

Winner of the Golden Quill and Heart of Excellence RWA awards

"Wynne has crafted a a beautiful short story guaranteed to warm your heart and make you sigh."

Kishan Paul, Second Wife Series

"...a wonderfully poignant holiday romantic tale that intertwines two love stories..."

Jersey Girls Book Reviews

"A lovely sweet romance!"

Book Addicts

Kathleen James has put her practical side away for once and looks forward to the perfect romantic evening: an intimate dinner with the man of her dreams—and an engagement ring. She is not prepared to hear that he wants to bring his grandmother back from Italy to live with him.

Dominic Lawrence has planned this marriage proposal for six months. Nothing can go wrong—until his Nonna calls. Now he must interrupt the tenderest night of Katie's life with the news that another woman will be under their roof.

When Antonia's sister dies, she finds herself longing to be back in the states. An Italian wartime bride from the '40s, she knows how precious love can be. Can her own story of an American soldier and a very special collie once again bring two hearts together at Christmas?

Paper Love (A Chicago Christmas #2)

http://aubreywynne.com/book/paper-love-a-chicago-christmas-2/

Bragg Medallion recipient, Golden Quill and Aspen Gold finalist

"This author has a knack for love stories that make your heart flutter."

Reads2Love Book Reviews

"Aubrey Wynne is a talented author weaving a descriptive setting, cultural details, historical facts, and inspirational romance into a delightful read."

Renate, Goodreads Review

Growing up in a Papua New Guinea mission, Joss Palmateer is a gentle soul with a unique view of life. Still adjusting to a new home in the U.S and the sudden loss of her mother, love is the last thing on her mind.

Sexy physical therapist, Ben Montgomery, meets his sister's friend and the sparks fly. He takes it as a silent challenge when she ignores his advances, but it's her extraordinary inner beauty that captures his heart.

With the help of a stray homing pigeon and an old origami legend, Ben sets an unwavering course of romance to win her love.

Merry Christmas, Henry (A Chicago Christmas #3)

http://aubreywynne.com/book/merry-christmas-henry-a-chicago-christmas-3/

Preditors and Editors Readers Choice Award

"Captivating Christmas Choice!"

Kindle Book Review

"Short, sweet, and stunning!"

Great Reads

Henry, a shy and talented artist, moonlights as a security guard at a museum and loses his heart to a beautiful, melancholy woman in a painting. As his obsession grows, he finds a kindred soul who helps him in his search for happiness. On Christmas Eve, Henry dares to take a chance on love and fulfill his dream.

Just for Sh*#$ and Giggles series

To Cast A Cliche (A Just for Sh*#$ and Giggles Short Story #1)
http://aubreywynne.com/book/to-cast-a-cliche/

"...a fractured fairy tale with humor and tongue in cheek...to use a cliché."

Amazon Reviewer

"Fairy tale lovers will delight in this short story... It's a fun read that will have you playing "count the cliches" until the cows come home."

Reads2Love

The evil Queen Lucinda exacts revenge on a royal poet by casting a spell of never-ending clichés upon the kingdom. Will the clever King Richard thwart his stepmother's magic and save the good people of Maxim? Test your literary knowledge and enjoy an entertaining spoof on fairytales.

Pete's Mighty Purty Privies (A Just for Sh*#$ and Giggles Short Story #2)

http://aubreywynne.com/book/petes-mighty-purty-privies/

Preditor's and Editors Readers Choice Award

Goodread's Top 100 Laugh Out Loud List

"The author has a gift for clarity and humor and I can't recommend this short story   enough. Hilarious!"

N.N. Light Book Reviews

"Expertly written and hysterical. You can't go wrong with this one."

Renea Mason, The Good Doctor trilogy

Pete McNutt needs customers for his new business. Spring has arrived and it's prime time Privy Season. After much consideration, he refines his sales pitch and heads to the monthly meeting of the Women's Library Association.

92549554R00109

Made in the USA
Lexington, KY
06 July 2018